Renaissance

A NOVEL

SUSAN FISH

RENAISSANCE

A NOVEL

PARACLETE PRESS
BREWSTER, MASSACHUSETTS

2023 First Printing

Renaissance: A Novel

ISBN 978-1-64060-873-3

Library of Congress Cataloging-in-Publication Data

Names: Fish, Susan, 1969- author.
Title: Renaissance : a novel / Susan Fish.
Description: Brewster, Massachusetts : Raven/Paraclete Press, [2023] | Summary: "Elizabeth Fane is on the cusp of 50, but instead of celebrating with her family, she is on a plane to Italy alone, leaving behind her husband, three adult sons, and the profound rift between them. In Italy Liz plans to prune olive trees at a convent, explore the city of Florence, and visit its ancient cathedrals. There she meets four women—five if you count the large painting of the Virgin Mary—with whom she converses regularly. While at first these conversations with the painting are ironic (and are always one-sided), eventually they turn to become another way for Liz to consider the rift between her and her family. Liz gradually reveals why she left home and sorts out what it will take for her to return. Renaissance is a coming-of-age story about a woman of a certain age — a novel about the end of motherhood as Liz steps out of longstanding domestic roles to find her own place in the world."—Provided by publisher. Identifiers: LCCN 2023022571 (print) | LCCN 2023022572 (ebook) | ISBN 9781640608733 (trade paperback) | ISBN 9781640608740 (epub) | ISBN 9781640608757 (pdf)
Subjects: LCSH: Self-realization in women--Fiction. | BISAC: FICTION / Women | FICTION / Family Life / General | LCGFT: Novels.
Classification: LCC PR9199.4.F564 R46 2023 (print) | LCC PR9199.4.F564 (ebook) | DDC 813/.6--dc23/eng/20230519
LC record available at https://lccn.loc.gov/2023022571
LC ebook record available at https://lccn.loc.gov/2023022572

10 9 8 7 6 5 4 3 2 1

Published by Paraclete Press
Brewster, Massachusetts
www.paracletepress.com

Printed in the United States of America

Midway on life's journey
I found myself alone in a dark wood
where the right way was lost.

—Dante Alighieri

Once upon a time, there was a piece of wood.

—Carlo Collodi

Allora, the Italians say. It is a multipurpose word, useful for many occasions. Someone asks directions: *allora*, first you take this street and then. . . .You are a young mother and your child is melting down in the art museum: *allora*, let's move on to the next room. . . . You are a judge on the Italian version of *Who Wants to be A Millionaire*, which is a team sport, and it is the ten-thousand-euro question: *allora*, let's get started. . . . You are a waiter in a trattoria. Your pencil is poised above your notepad and you look expectantly at your customers. *Allora* . . .

In Canada we say "So . . ." a lot, but *allora* is a soothing word, suggesting that whatever is to come can be managed, a word that encourages speaker and listener to roll up their sleeves and try to sort it out. There may be a thousand blue pieces in this jigsaw puzzle, and they may be scattered on the floor now, may be missing more than a few essential pieces, may be drenched after a sudden spill of wine or perhaps the catastrophic spill of blood.

You may fear that it will never fit together again, that you can never make the picture right, and you may well be right, but, *allora*, let's begin.

RENAISSANCE

1

I SAT FORTY THOUSAND FEET ABOVE THE ATLANTIC, all the blue puzzle pieces of that ocean. I had tried to sleep but we were bad sleepers, our family, unable to let ourselves go while in motion, let alone in public. I envied my seatmate, a man in a suit who had put on a dark eye mask and fallen asleep even before we left Toronto. His breathing was steady and rhythmic. I couldn't sleep, more than a bit concerned about what would happen if I did, if I confused him for Russ, and woke up with my head on his shoulder.

I watched the electronic map on the back of the seat in front of me as we gradually arced our way across the world. As the hours wore on, the cabin lights were slowly dimmed, and people found space to settle themselves, limbs splayed, all around the cabin.

The thought played in an endless loop in my head: *Would this solve anything? Would I ever be able to go home again?*

Finally, somewhere over the Irish Sea, around three in the morning our time at home, my long blinks and head falling forward became a sort of imperative, my need for sleep overriding everything else.

It hurt to wake up about an hour later. My neck ached, reminding me of the awful fatigue I'd had when the boys were small: being awakened in the night was fundamentally different from waking up with your own body's signals, even if the hour for waking was the same. It hurt, too, as it always did when I woke up the last few months: even high above the earth, nothing about my situation had changed.

What woke me was a voice, scratchy over the plane's intercom, the captain's voice. As I tried to register what he was saying,

I realized that people had opened blinds to reveal merciless sunlight, and flight attendants were already beginning to serve breakfast. All around me, people were waking up, strangers strangely intimate in yesterday's clothes and faces softened by sleep.

Strong headwinds, the captain said, had delayed our ocean crossing, and we would be arriving in Frankfurt around eleven local time. My hands began to sweat: my connecting plane was scheduled to depart at ten-thirty.

My seatmate swore, pulling off his eye mask with a vicious snap of the elastic.

I wasn't sure, never having flown alone before, what the protocol was when it came to privacy between strangers jammed so closely into intimate proximity. I gave him a sympathetic eye roll.

"Abu Dhabi," he said. For one confused moment, I thought it was another curse word or an incantation, but then I understood.

"Florence," I said, naming my own destination.

He shook his head as if to dismiss my concerns. "They'll get you there this afternoon. Me? Depending on how full the red eye is, I might not even get there tomorrow. Damn!"

"Work?" I asked as the flight attendant approached the row in front of us.

"Why else go to Abu Dhabi," he said as we settled our trays. "You?"

I was grateful that the flight attendant interrupted us at that point, pouring drinks and passing our food to us, because there were two stories about why I was going to Italy: the story everyone knew, and the true story only I knew.

Once when I was in high school, I had taken a train to Ottawa, and on the way there a university student had invited me to go into the washroom with him to smoke up. I hadn't been interested in the particulars of his offer but I had liked the thought that I could be anyone on a train, even a girl who casually did drugs, and when he came back, slightly glassy-eyed and with all the time in the world, I had told him things I would never tell my friends back at home.

But I had a different story to tell now. I wondered whether I could tell it to Mr. Abu Dhabi, someone else I would never meet again. I could tell him of the ripping within me, the violation, the visceral pain.

But I wasn't seventeen anymore and he wasn't high. No one wanted to hear this story of mine, to be trapped behind breakfast trays and insufficient legroom by a stranger's tears.

All of this passed through my mind before he raised a forkful of airline eggs, wishing me "Bon appétit."

"I'm going to volunteer at a convent," I said, sticking to the simple version everyone knew before he forgot his question.

He jolted, shifting in his chair, as if to sit more upright. "You're a nun?" he said.

I laughed. It was not that different from what my mother had said when she heard what I was going to do. "No, I'm not. I'll be helping with their gardens."

I could tell from his expression that gardening was only slightly less foreign to him than nuns, although he did relax again in his seat. I knew only a bit about gardening—although it had perhaps saved my sanity the last few months—but this trip was not the same as working in my own safe yard.

It was what I was going to do and a way of easily telling my story. But there was another story beneath that one.

2

The story I didn't tell—the complicated one—began two years ago when our organization's bookkeeper came into my office, closed the door, sat in the chair across from mine, told me she was leaving, and why.

I had long practice in keeping my face neutral when people disclosed their stories.

I knew her situation. She had four school-aged children and her husband had lost his job a few months before. The sole family income was her work as a bookkeeper.

She kept talking and I sat quietly listening.

Because I was the executive director of the organization, *dealing with complicated* was a big part of my job description, but it had already been a long day with more challenges than usual. I had woken up in the night and stayed awake thinking about one of our clients who was in crisis. That morning I'd had meetings with two other clients in challenging situations and our receptionist had told me we were low on supplies and she had no idea why. There were people who were mad at me as I had always known there would be, as there always were with those in leadership. The only thing I hadn't banked on were people who were mad at me for their mistaken ideas of what we stood for.

I turned to Jenn. "I want you to stay with us," I said. "You make a big difference here. And you don't use all the accounting acronyms our old bookkeeper did. If I have to go back to FE versus OE, I will possibly lose my mind. It's hard enough keeping up with my kids and their texting. I'm not sure I can do it here."

Jenn returned my words with a soft smile.

I continued, hopeful. "What you just told me makes me want to keep you all the more."

"But I can't, can I?" she said.

I didn't know. My job was to know all the policies and bylaws, the mission, vision, and values, and to lead our organization, to be its mother duck, its queen bee. Normally I loved that role, but sometimes—like this moment—ideals, values, ethics, and pragmatism collided. There was no simple answer.

So much of our culture has done us a disservice. Take cowboy movies. The hero in the white hat. The moustache-twirling villain. We don't realize the complexities—the good people who make wrenching choices, the complicated reasons any of us do anything. The situations in which no choice feels good, in which no choice *is* good.

3

We came through the clouds and Frankfurt was under heavy gray skies, heavier even than Toronto's when we left. It was exactly what I had pictured Germany being like: colorless, industrial, and ugly. I sent Russ and the boys a quick text as we taxied to the terminal to let them know I had arrived.

In the lengthy line for customs, I found myself intrigued as I watched the agents who faced us through a long glass wall while passengers turned toward them. I wondered how it worked: did they randomly ask passengers for a more thorough check? Were they racially profiling? I began to look at passengers in the line ahead of me, imagining what I would do in a customs agent role. At first I looked for signs: did people's shoes match the rest of their outfit? Were they sweating just a bit too much? Then as we turned a corner in the maze of lineups, I remembered how I'd once heard that that people who checked for counterfeit bills and coins spent much of their time studying the real thing. But how could you know when a person was real or counterfeit?

A woman with hard eyes assessed me, a human X-ray. I suppose she found me credible, harmless or both. She spoke to me in English, as though somehow she saw me completely.

After I had been approved to enter Europe, I found the Air Canada desk where they began with the familiar "Hello, *bonjour.*" They worried me only briefly by musing about sending me to Rome before finding me a spot on the next Florence flight, replacing someone who had taken one of the seats on the ten-thirty flight. Mr. Abu Dhabi had been right. I hoped he would have similar success wherever he was.

Sitting under the convoluted metal tubes that covered the airport ceiling, I watched planes taxiing in and out until they announced it was time to board a shuttle that took us into the late-winter chill of the afternoon toward our plane.

4

I COULD ALSO SAY MY COMPLICATED STORY BEGAN many years earlier, on another chilly winter day when I saw a sign on a telephone pole in my neighborhood.

At the time I had wanted a fourth child—if it could be a girl—but Russ thought that would extend to a fifth and a sixth child. He showed me tables and statistics demonstrating the low likelihood of having a girl after three boys. But ever since our first son was born, I had been a baby person—I loved the way a newborn molded itself to your arms, the way they smelled of yeasty milk and freshness.

Still pondering the idea of a fourth child, I saw that sign on a telephone pole asking for volunteers to work with seniors at a community services organization in our neighborhood. It wasn't a new baby but I thought I could try it out as a home for my nurturing energy.

"One rule," Russ had said with a smile when I told him I was considering volunteering. "They aren't kittens, Liz. You aren't bringing any home with you."

I hadn't, of course. And I had enjoyed the work even if seniors smelled nothing at all like delicious babies. It had gotten me out of the house and gave me an outlet for caregiving twice a week. But then came the day when the executive director suddenly had to go home with the stomach flu and she handed me the literal and figurative keys to the building. I hadn't realized until then that my parenting skills were quite so transferrable. Nor had I been aware that I'd been unconsciously job-shadowing the executive director for months so that I knew exactly what to do. I went home with a profound sense of satisfaction that the program had gone smoothly, largely thanks to my work.

I knew the feeling. During my first pregnancy I had thought I couldn't be The Mother, that I was The Kid. But when they put Timothy into my arms, nothing had ever felt so purely right. I clearly remember peering into that small, scrunched-up face and thinking, *Oh, I can totally be* your *mother*. That was followed by a period of postpartum bliss, despite my new parent fears. I liked children before I had my boys, but my heart found depths I had never dreamed of before the babies were mine. At times it felt almost idolatrous and all-consuming.

It had only been the one afternoon at the senior center, but the next time I went in to volunteer, I talked with the executive director, Karin, about the experience. I sat across from Karin's desk and realized that I wanted to be the person volunteers came to with such situations, the person who gave wise counsel or encouraging words or jokes. I wanted to be the one offering the Kleenex and the performance evaluations, the one working with the board and the budgets. To her credit, Karin didn't laugh when I told her. Instead, she let me work closely with her and eventually hired me as the volunteer coordinator. She was my reference when I applied to a graduate program and then again when I graduated and applied for the role as an executive director at another organization.

I still thought of the organization I headed up as my "new" organization, even though it had been more than ten years since I left the senior center. Accounting acronyms aside, it had been the right role for me. There were sleepless nights of second-guessing myself and seasons where my work felt flat or when I felt tinges of cynicism about whether what we did made a difference. But I knew how to avoid the turn toward compassion fatigue and burnout. I *did* love being the person offering the Kleenex and leading the team. I loved working with the board on a common purpose, even when we clashed or struggled for funds. It felt a bit like conducting an orchestra and bringing very different instruments and voices into harmony.

And then came the day that led me to flee to Italy.

5

THE LITTLE SCHOOL BUS OF AN AIRPLANE CREAKED and popped up the Frankfurt runway and within a few short minutes, we had shed the gray winter chill to fly through brilliant sunshine. By the time we were flying over the Italian Alps, I had learned that my seatmate, an older man in a blazer and a mid-winter tan, lived in California with his second wife—"A terrible mistake"—and that he was on one of his frequent returns to Florence. I listened carefully when he offered suggestions: when you get gelato, listen for what the Italians are ordering; don't talk with the street sellers; be sure to go to the opera; don't eat raw olives if you don't want to be sick. I thanked him with a *grazie*.

Before I knew it, we were descending into a green world dotted with red tile roofs, terracotta everywhere, and a brilliant blue river undulating back and forth. As we came lower still, I could see terraced hillsides and trees and more red roofs, and then suddenly we were bumping along, earthbound.

The airport was smaller than the bus depot at home, and smokier. Miraculously my luggage arrived with my flight and was in my possession within five minutes. I stepped out into the cool sunshine, found a queue for taxis and, in awkward Italian, told my driver the name of the convent where I was staying: *Le Suore Stabilite nella Carità*. The driver nodded and I hoped my six weeks of language classes had provided me with enough Italian to find my way.

Tired though I was—exhausted, in fact, as if gravity had increased its force to maximum—I kept my eyes open, not wanting to miss a thing, including what started to seem like my inevitable death from collision with the dozens of Vespas that leaned a perilously hard left in every roundabout, then darted in and out of traffic as they streamed beside us on highways and overpasses, along winding narrow streets and hills.

As we passed ugly apartment buildings and billboards advertising alcohol and strippers, I wondered what would happen if I hated Italy, if I had spent all this time and money on a trip, banking on it being an interesting but safe place, only to find it disturbingly alien. An ambulance passed us but then got stuck in traffic just ahead of us. I felt anxious for whoever awaited its help.

Then, as we began ascending a long hill, I noticed palm trees flanking the boulevard, as if this were California. I saw a couple posing for wedding photos in a park. I saw people greet one another with kisses on both cheeks. I saw a man balancing a precariously tall stack of shoeboxes on one forearm. My taxi driver pointed, and I looked—it was, impossibly, inevitably, the roof of the Duomo dominating the skyline in the distance. My mood lifted as we climbed the hill.

We rose higher and higher until finally the driver stopped, the car idling outside tall wrought iron gates. We had passed dozens of similar gates as we crept up the winding roads, but this was apparently the convent. I crawled out and fumbled for my credit card. The driver opened the trunk and handed me my bags. I paid him and said "Grazie" and then looked at the gates, unsure how to open them. Back on his side of the car, the driver called to me and pointed to a small buzzer next to the locked gates. I mimed my thanks as he drove away, and then I pushed the buzzer, hoping he was right.

"*Sì?*" came a woman's voice almost instantly.

"*Mi chiamo* Liz Fane. I'm Elizabeth Fane."

There was a pause and then a click and the gate began to swing open. I walked in and stood looking up at the house: it was an ochre-yellow stucco villa with a red tiled roof. The entire front yard of the house was paved with cobblestones. An image of Maria in *The Sound of Music* came to mind, and I stifled a laugh that was potentially hysterical with fatigue at the thought, hoping I would not be called upon to make dresses out of drapery. The gate closed behind me with a clang that startled me.

I picked up my bags, thinking of our youngest son, Gil, last September as he had walked away from us into his ivy-covered college residence for the first time. I had sat in the car, both wanting him to look back and not to turn at the same time. In the end, he did turn and gave us a wave, smiling broadly, a smile that let us know he would be fine.

The front door of the convent opened, and a woman stood at the door wearing a powder-blue habit—I supposed it was a habit—and thick black eyebrows. She looked at me the way I looked at our cats when they acted as though they needed special invitations to come inside.

I hurried up the steps and offered an apology. "*Scusi*," I said, getting close to the end of my Italian much faster than I had expected. She began to speak in a torrent of Italian and I held up my hands as if to say she had won the language contest. She pointed her index finger sharply, miming that I should wait, and rustled away down the corridor. I didn't dare move, but I put my bags down on the polished terracotta tiles and let my eyes adjust after the brightness of the outside world.

In a moment, the nun returned with a second nun, this one far younger and smaller, with enormous clear brown eyes. She looked up at me with a shy smile. "Elizabetta?"

Ay-leez-a-beh-ta, she pronounced my name. I said it again in my head and I wondered whether I could forever and always and at home in Waterloo County be called Elizabetta.

I nodded that yes, that was me.

The young nun pointed to what looked like a schoolroom and said, in English, "For the meals." I felt relief to hear my own language and I laughed.

The older nun cleared her throat and led me into a wood-paneled elevator so tiny it only had room for one of my suitcases. The smaller nun took my other suitcase, pointed at a stone staircase and then upward. "I meet you," she said. The elevator doors closed, and I felt it begin to creep slowly upward, certain there were nuns in the basement riding bicycles to make the elevator rise. I realized I had just handed off my passport, contact lenses, toothbrush and camera to be stuck in this slow-rising coffin with a beetle-browed nun who apparently didn't speak a word of English. I smiled at her and she did something with her face back at me.

The door opened just as I thought of the word *claustrophobia*, and when the little nun was there, smiling at me, it felt like a familiar face. I followed the two nuns who led me through a labyrinth of hallways before opening a door that led to an outdoor walkway.

I was entirely stopped by my first view of what lay behind the convent. Just below us were terraces with raised formal gardens. Sloping down and away from the building and the terraces was an orchard of ancient trees clad in silvery green leaves. Dividing these trees were two long rows of enormous black-green evergreens, unlike anything we had in Canada. In the distance were soft hills and red roofs and a glimpse of blue, perhaps the river I had seen from the plane. It took my breath away.

The older nun cleared her throat again and it was clear she saw me as a dawdler, but then she must see this view every day. It struck me that I too would now see this view every day. She handed me a pair of keys and indicated that I should open the door at the end of the covered walkway.

We entered a common room with furniture that was less Renaissance-villa and more 1970s suburbia in style. The young nun pointed out the small kitchen and the bathroom as we went along and then we entered a hallway of bedrooms. The older nun stopped at the second bedroom door and waved a hand to indicate I should open it with the other key she had given me.

The young nun followed me into the room while the older nun stayed in the hallway. With a quick glance toward the door, the young nun pointed at her chest and looked up at me. "I am called Salvia," she said. Then, in a louder voice she said, "Dinner is serve at eight o'clock." With that she joined the other nun, and they went back to the main building, leaving me alone.

My ears rang with the silence, and I started to feel shaky with fatigue and on the verge of tears. There were two single beds draped in orange coverlets my grandmother might have used. I sat down on the bed closest to the window, and then the other one, as though I were Goldilocks trying to find the one that was just right. I was so tired that any horizontal surface felt compelling. I wanted so badly to lie down and fall asleep, but everyone had warned me that I had to resist jet lag, that I needed to force myself into the new time zone.

I looked up and saw that facing the beds was a painting in an ornate gold frame that almost filled the entire wall. A portrait of a young woman in a blue dress, a halo illuminating her head, a head she tilted equivocally, as if asking why I was there. It was a good question. Right now I couldn't remember why.

The room smelled a bit like a library. I felt panicky suddenly: *Why had I thought this would help? And what if it didn't?* The air in the room felt close and I decided to open the windows.

Huge and reaching to the ceiling, they were complicated to open. Behind the windows were outdoor shutters that swung open as I pushed them—and there was the view that had stopped me short as I crossed the walkway. I decided to go for a walk in that landscape, and to panic and unpack later.

An outside door and then a set of winding metal stairs along the outside of the building took me down to the ground level.

For a long time, I stood on the gravel terrace and just looked and looked in every direction. Behind me was the villa and around me were carefully sculpted hedges surrounding the formal gardens that were empty of plants in the winter. The land fell away from the villa, dropping into the sea of silvery green I now realized was the olive grove.

The tall evergreens I'd seen from the walkway looked even more impressive and foreboding now as I stood at their feet. They rose higher than the villa, though they grew far below it. Cypresses. These were tall, ancient trees, and they stood like guards on either side of a pathway that led down and away from the villa.

I descended through the gardens and into the olive trees and beyond to the tall stone obelisks that marked the entrance to a passageway between the rows of the terrible, majestic cypresses. I kept following the path, down its stairs made of old stone, even as I regretted leaving my sweater in my room. It had been cool in the afternoon sunshine, but in this dark shade, there was a significant chill.

I could hear traffic below me, with Vespas and motorcycles hugging the side of this ancient mountainside. My legs were stiff and still tired from the plane, but I decided I would walk to the bottom of the property and then back up to my room. Near the bottom I found myself not at a lower wall as I had expected but in a kind of clearing where the cypresses formed a wide circle about me. Whether it was a circle of protection or a dead end, I couldn't yet tell.

6

Late last fall I had spent endless hours trying to sort it all out, trying to make a coherent narrative out of what had happened, trying to think about what I could have done differently, where I had erred, hitting a dead end at every turn.

Earlier in the year, Gil going to college had left us with the proverbial empty nest. Where I'd felt a bit of relief when Tim went off to university and mild panic when Jackson moved out, I experienced grief when Gil left last September. The house was far too quiet when I woke up every morning, and all the more so because Russ's vice president at the insurance company finally retired, freeing Russ to do work he had wanted to do for years.

There were huge bonuses to having the boys gone, of course. A tank of gas lasted us three weeks and I had to make bran muffins after a carton of milk had turned—when before milk had never lasted long enough to go sour. We reverted to sleeping naked again after more than twenty years of careful, familial modesty.

But in the weeks after Gil left, I felt greed in my heart as I watched young parents for whom parenthood lay before them rather than behind them. I thought of the dairy board commercials featuring families with older parents who were weary at the fact that their middle-aged children still lived at home, the commercials that exhorted the parents to stop cooking with cheese if they wanted their children to move out. I idly wondered what would have happened if I had cooked *more* with cheese.

Finally, when I saw a book on empty nest syndrome at a church rummage sale, I sandwiched it between two classic novels and paid for it before anyone could tease me or even ask questions about how I was doing without my kids.

There was a quiz at the start of the book—assessing whether the reader truly was in the throes of empty nest syndrome. My answers told me I was in the mild category. The book advised that I take up new hobbies or adopt a pet. I turned the page, both reassured and hoping the advice got better.

On the next page, I read words that sprang off the page as if they were the words of Jesus in a red-letter Bible: "Midway on life's journey I found myself alone in a dark wood where the right way was lost."

It was something like when Timothy was born: I knew, instinctively, that this was completely right and true. The words expressed much of how I felt but I had no idea how important these words would be when the real grief hit. Still, I looked up the quote. It was the beginning of Dante's *Inferno*, written after the Italian poet had been exiled from his beloved city of Florence.

A month later when I was violently ripped out of my happy life, there were no words, no simple term like *empty nest syndrome* to describe what happened. Now in my fiftieth year, all I had to cling to were Dante's words when, like the poet, I was suddenly sent into exile.

7

It was dark when I woke up, jolted awake by the sound of voices outside my room. It took a moment for me to realize where I was and then I was afraid I had missed dinner. I looked over at my phone and it was only seven-thirty. I had tried so hard to stay awake after my walk, but apparently it hadn't worked. I looked up at the painting on the wall and I couldn't decipher the expression on the woman's face.

I stepped out of my room, still dazed and disoriented.

"Hey," came a voice. "I didn't know you were here yet. *Benvenuto!* Welcome!"

I found the source of the voice—it was a young woman sitting on top of the counter in the kitchenette. She was all arms and legs in a tank top and jeans, a tattooed vine twining down one arm, blonde hair pulled up on top of her head. She jumped up and shook my hand. Her hand was rough.

"I'm Honey," she said, and gestured to a tiny woman with dark dreadlocks sitting cross-legged on the floor in front of the mini-fridge, looking like she was playing Jenga with the contents. "And this is Cecy."

"I'm—" I couldn't manage Elizabetta. Not yet—"Liz."

"Did they call you Leeza?" Honey asked. "The nuns? They call me Miele."

"Elizabetta."

"And they put you in the room with the picture I like to call *Our Lady of Perpetual Constipation*?" Cecy said, speaking at last. "I'm in *Of Course I'm a Virgin, How Dare You.*"

"Cecy!" Honey said.

"It could be worse. She could be in *Jesus, Bloody Jesus* like you."

"Sorry," said Honey, "We've been here awhile. You ever hear of Stendahl syndrome?"

I shook my head.

"People go to too many museums and they get overloaded with art and they have a breakdown. It's kind of like that for Cecy, only it's an excess of nuns. And their paintings."

"So many Jesuses, so many Marys," said Cecy, managing to close the fridge door after several attempts.

"How long have you been here?" I asked.

"Since just after New Year's," Honey said. "We were in France before that. We spent New Year's in Nice. It was nice."

I restrained my laughter when I quickly realized this was apparently not offered as a joke.

"You picked a good time to come," Honey said. "They've finally decided we can work outside. This week we pruned the rose bushes, but up until now it's been sharpening tools, sterilizing bottles, and putting labels on them. Next week we get to start pruning trees and planting gardens."

"Just when I have to leave," said Cecy, wrapping her arms around Honey from behind. Just then a buzzer sounded overhead. "Dinner bell. I hope you're hungry. I'll say one thing for these babes—they know how to cook. I've put on fifteen pounds since I've been here."

I followed them out the door and across the rooftop walkway to the main villa. If what Cecy said were true, she must have been emaciated to begin with. I paused in the middle of the walkway and looked out between the arches into the velvety blackness. The hills were dotted with light as if the stars had come down to touch the earth.

"We had to scoot across here in January," said Honey, holding the door to the main villa open for me. We descended the curving stone staircase to the dining room the little nun had pointed out earlier. It reminded me of an old-fashioned schoolroom with high windows. We sat at the only one of the small narrow tables that was set for dinner, although they were all draped with faded pink linen tablecloths.

Cecy had not been exaggerating about the nuns' cooking abilities. I wrongly assumed that the third course—the pasta—was the main course but it was followed by platters of pan-fried whitefish and bowls of green beans and potatoes, and then a cheese course and fruit. It was served by a nun with a face like a wizened apple who urged us to "*Mangia! Mangia!*" I had been hungry beforehand, but by the time I finished the fish and potatoes, I couldn't find space for a single bite of cheese, though I looked longingly at the great wedges. I didn't know what the nun was saying, but I could tell from her tone and face that she was chastising my lack of intestinal fortitude.

As we ate, I listened as Honey and Cecy told me how they had come to be at the convent. Honey had spent a year with a traveling carnival—*not* a circus, she explained—and she had picked almonds in California. She met Cecy in France where Cecy was busking—she was a juggler—and Honey persuaded her to come to Florence to help out at this convent.

"If she had told me their name," Cecy said, rolling her eyes. "I wouldn't have come."

Then there was me: nonprofit executive director with my four-bedroom house in Waterloo, my insurance executive husband, three sons, two cats and one broken heart. The beauty and the jet lag had kept the pain at bay for the afternoon, but now it flooded back.

Even as I worked to eat more than I thought I could, I tried to take in all the information Honey and Cecy were offering me throughout the meal.

"Don't ask if you can have coffee at supper," Honey said, picking up the last of the cheese with her fingers. "No one in Italy ever drinks coffee after noon. You can make some back in Lemonland if you want some."

"Lemonland?"

"Our dorm. That's what it's called. It's built over the *limonaia* where they store their lemon trees for the winter. The girl who was staying here when we got here, she called it that, so we call it that."

I finished my wine. It was the best glass of red wine I'd ever had, and I said so.

"It comes from a monastery near here," Honey said. "The convents and monasteries all trade stuff—honey, wine, olive oil. . . ."

"Blow jobs," added Cecy.

I was already on overload and didn't have it in me to deal with this kind of conversation. I needed this place to be a good place, a safe haven, and Cecy was wrecking that. "I need to get some sleep," I said, recognizing that I was exhausted and that the wine was adding to my fatigue. "What do I need to know for tomorrow?"

"Breakfast is at seven-thirty. Even on Sundays. Tomorrow you can do whatever you want and then on Monday morning, the English-speaking nun will give us our orders at breakfast."

"Is it just the three of us staying here?" I asked. Somehow I had pictured being part of a larger group.

"There are a couple of paying guests—someone at a conference and a couple on their honeymoon. I heard there might be someone else coming after Cecy leaves—but maybe that's you—and then a whole busload of tourists."

"Are we allowed to—" *Fraternize?*— "talk to the paying guests?"

"We always say hi to them," Honey said. "There aren't any *rule*-rules about it."

"There just haven't been any really attractive ones," said Cecy, cutting another slice of cheese.

"Oh, and if you wake up super-early, the nuns say we're always welcome to join their morning singalong in the chapel. At six-thirty."

As I walked back to my room, I recognized what I really wanted was to stretch out my muscles in a bathtub, in my own bathtub, which was literally on the other side of the world. Here there was no tub, only a cramped enameled metal shower stall. Everything struck me as deeply foreign, and I felt petulant and aching with dislocation.

When had I stopped welcoming change? Gil had done an exchange term to Australia in high school—to Brisbane—and he had been disappointed by how things hadn't been as different as he had expected. He'd hoped for a Dr. Seussian landscape, something otherworldly, I think. But this was somehow *more* different than I expected and I didn't have the resources to cope with that on top of everything else.

I called Russ in tears after I showered, when I felt as if I was on another planet where the force of gravity was that much stronger. I recognized that I had jet lag, recognized how profoundly tired I was from the two days' travel and the lost night's sleep, but I also knew I didn't want to be here. I thought the words to myself—*I don't want to be here*—but I didn't dare speak them aloud, even to Russ, for fear I would be entirely undone, packing myself into a taxi that night and onto another sleepless plane ride.

I had told myself I wouldn't be far from home—that Jackson was an eight-hour car ride away at school and I was an eight-hour plane ride away from home—but now I knew that was only technically true, that it didn't include waiting in airports, negotiating customs, and riding in buses and taxis. Then, too, in this state I even couldn't let myself look at the fact that I couldn't exactly go home easily anyhow.

All I said to Russ was "Everything is different here," but he heard the ache in my voice and calmly and kindly said the words *culture shock*. I clung to those words as I slid into bed and the sheets were cold and smelled different from my sheets at home, and the gilded portrait on the wall seemed alien and Catholic and smug.

"*Parli inglese*?" I asked the woman in the portrait. She didn't answer. *Our Lady of Perpetual Constipation*, Cecy had called her. After I turned out the light, I realized it was a picture of Mary, the mother of Jesus.

But as tired as I was, I lay awake in bed, as I had for months at home, staring at the ceiling. I drifted off to sleep eventually and awoke to the sound of Honey and Cecy giggling and trying to be quiet as they came in. Maybe it was the convent and Cecy's excess of nuns or that I was half asleep, but I thought to myself that we were like children sent off to boarding school.

I had not exactly been sent off, though. I had sent myself.

8

I'd never heard anyone suggest that going to Italy in February was desirable in the least. Particularly to work on a farm, as my mother called it. Most particularly to work on a farm run by nuns, as my mother pointedly said.

It could be argued that ticket prices to Italy in late February were cheaper, that it was low season so the hordes of tourists would be significantly smaller and fewer, but even when I weakly offered those explanations as I told friends I was going to Italy, they invariably looked puzzled.

When someone thinks about Tuscany, they think of late summer when the sun beats down on the red-tiled roofs, when gelato and naps become necessities rather than luxuries, and when there is a general sense of the sheer abundance for which Italy is known. Think Italy and you think opera, think pasta, think rolling hills and flowing wine.

Many of my friends had gone to Italy—some on cruise ships, some on tours—but there were reasons they went during high season. It certainly wasn't because any of them wanted to be standing in long lines, buying monstrously expensive bottles of water just to stay hydrated. No, there was a perfect season for everything, and Italy's perfect season was late summer. It was worth the crowds to be there at its peak, my friend Joanna argued. It was like going to Florida in January or driving through the Adirondacks in the fall. There were reasons to do it that way.

If you wanted to be a little different, you could go to Italy in the shoulder seasons, as my travel agent called them, spring or fall. It wouldn't be quite so perfect but you would avoid the heat and some of the crowds, although the prices were virtually the same.

The idea to come to Italy and the convent had arrived during our annual holiday kickoff party three months before. We had hosted the party for more than twenty years on the last Saturday in November, as a way of redeeming November and making sure we saw everyone before the Christmas madness began. Our friends had come to expect it and didn't even need invitations anymore.

All that month I had been on autopilot, numb and going through the motions. On the surface our life was unchanged from what it had been before. Underneath, though, everything had changed. It made me think of early pregnancy, the profound excruciating fatigue caused by something smaller than a lentil. "I'm making ears," I would tell myself when I was pregnant and had trouble staying awake. "I'm making a whole entire human being." I would think of the princess and the pea, the delicate girl who could not sleep despite a hundred mattresses between her and the small pea, her insomnia proving she was a real princess. But this tiny pea was now stuck deep beneath the mattresses of my life. That I somehow shouldn't be able to feel it and that perhaps this made me a sort of princess gave me precisely zero comfort.

But I had done the party so many times before that I could do it almost without thinking, double-checking by following the dictates of the spreadsheet Russ had set up that told us who to invite, what to buy, and when to make food.

On the night of the party, Russ's executive assistant, Eva, stood before me holding out a platter covered with slices of bread cut into triangles, drizzled with greenish oil and sprinkled with salt. She insisted I take a piece. People invariably wanted to bring something to our party: it was how we stocked up on wine and how we had discovered all sorts of snacks for our pantry over the years.

As I had appeased my mother by eating her green bean casserole the week before, and as I had forced myself through every meal for weeks, I took a small slice of bread and began to go through the motions. The greenness of spring exploded in my mouth—a fresh explosion of pepper mingled with the creaminess of butter. Eva had already turned to offer the bread and oil to someone else, but I followed her and asked if I might have more.

"I know," she said. "It's addictive, isn't it?"

The oil hit the back of my throat and made me cough, but I ate a third piece.

"I won't be able to go back to the stuff they sell in the stores here," Eva said.

"Where did you get it?" I asked.

"Martha—my daughter Martha—spent a month harvesting olives at a convent in Italy this fall. It's from there. They said if she brought them a litre of maple syrup, they would trade her for a litre of olive oil. So I sent her with two litres of maple syrup. And even still, I'm rationing the oil for special occasions like tonight."

I took a fourth piece of bread and mopped oil off the plate. "How did that come about? Working at an olive grove?"

I listened as she explained that the convent was called the Sisters of Stability and Charity—"Unlike my sisters," Eva joked. People could come to stay and work with the nuns in their gardens and olive groves for a minimum of two weeks and a maximum of twelve weeks for a shockingly low fee which included room and board.

When she said their name and that it was possible to stay there and help them prune their trees, I recognized that it was a lifeline, one I needed to grab. Stability and charity. That was all I'd ever wanted.

9

I WOKE THE FIRST MORNING IN ITALY TO THE SOUND OF BELLS that had an ancient clang that was different from bells I had heard before. There was no question of where I was. I had dreamed about the nun with the beetle brow stroking my hair. I looked over at the Virgin Mary on the wall. She held her hands open, raised toward the sky, her head surrounded by its halo of gold. In the light of day, her inscrutable expression said she was accepting of whatever might come next.

Could I do likewise? I had signed on for fifty days of waking up in this bed and going to sleep in this bed. Books I read said it took forty days to form a new habit, but I had wanted more than that. I had wanted all the time I needed. Now fifty days seemed infinitely long. Could I do it? Could I stay until Easter?

As I made myself get out of bed, I told myself that what I felt were nerves. I reminded myself that if it didn't work out, I could always go home early. And then, my stomach curdled again. Because going home didn't have any feeling of going *home.*

I stepped into the hallway to use the washroom, and I could hear either Cecy or Honey snoring. Nice, I told myself, I could go there. Nice was nice, they said.

After a night's sleep and in the light of day, the washroom seemed less cramped, less foreign. I looked in the mirror. It was small and only framed my head and shoulders, like a kind of portrait that only showed a part of me. It didn't, for instance, show my C-section scars or my stretch marks. My face looked paler than usual against my dark hair. But even in Italy, I was still me, and I'd brought my troubles with me. And now I had a whole empty day ahead of me before I could be distracted by pruning olive trees. I looked at myself in the mirror and told myself I could do it—that at least I could try. I wasn't sure I was convinced, so I tilted my head like the portrait of Mary accepting her future, took a deep breath and opened the door to face whatever came next.

It was Sunday morning, which perhaps explained the abundance of bells that continued to echo back and forth across the valley. I stopped on the walkway to look out at the early morning, the light almost purple over the hills.

I had heard there was an English Church in Florence, but I had decided to let myself sleep until I woke up, and give myself the day off church, the way I had after each of the kids were born and as I had after I'd had the flu one time. Whether this passage was more like giving birth or recovering from sickness, I wasn't sure. All I knew was that I would take the day slowly.

As I turned the corner to descend the marble stairs, I could suddenly hear signs of life—voices and footsteps and clattering pots.

There was only one other person at breakfast, a young man who had already nearly finished his meal. I nodded to him and sat down at the table from the night before, unsure whether I was allowed to move tables, and lacking the language to ask.

I fiddled with the small foil-wrapped pats of jam and butter on my table, wishing I had not left my phone in my room. The young man at the other table looked settled, like he knew the routine or even that he belonged. I wondered whether Cecy had met him and judged him not attractive enough.

A nun I had not seen before came toward me bringing two metal pitchers and indicated I should pour them into my cup simultaneously, steaming milk and dense black coffee. I obeyed her instructions and then sipped my milky, nutty coffee as she spoke in Italian to the man, words flowing together like the coffee and milk so that I couldn't separate them into language I could understand.

At home, I would not pay the least attention to a person at the next table in a restaurant unless he disturbed or interrupted me in some way. Because there I was in the midst of my life, engaged with so much that I would automatically tune out the rest. Here I was free to observe anything and everything. In fact it was a relief to have new things to see, a blank slate, a new day. I noticed the man's tee shirt, for instance, adorned with a drawing of two cats.

"*Buona giornata*," the man said to me after the nun strode off into the kitchen and as he rose from his table and gathered his thick calendar under his arm.

When I smiled and tried to say the same words to him, he smiled back. "English?" he asked in what was clearly a Midwestern American accent.

Sono canadese. I had learned to say that much. *Non parlo italiano.* But I didn't even need to try to *parlo italiano.* "Canadian," I said.

"Is this your first time here?" he said, gesturing around the room.

"My first time in Italy."

"Lucky you." When I asked what had brought him to the convent, he told me he had been presenting an astronomy paper at a conference at the Galileo observatory which apparently sat just higher up the hill. He said that our convent had once been a villa owned by a friend of Galileo's, that Galileo had come to the villa for visits when he was under house arrest.

Galileo, a neighbor before eight in the morning? Suddenly the world which had felt so large and foreign the day before had a touch of enchantment.

I asked about his shirt.

He looked down. "It's a physics thing," he said. "It's a thought experiment. Schrödinger's Cat. If you had a cat in a box, quantum mechanics says until you look in the box, you just don't know if it is alive or not, so the cat is both alive and dead simultaneously."

I thought of my cats. I hoped they were alive in my absence.

"Here," he said, reaching into his pocket. "I'm leaving today and I won't be using my last bus ticket. Would you like it?"

"Thank you," I said. "*Grazie.* Where do I catch the bus into the city?"

The nun strode back with a small basket of bread and placed it on my table. I took a piece and spread butter and apricot jam on it as the astronomer explained how I could get into the city proper. He rummaged in his case and took out a map of the Florence bus routes. "We're here—" The convent was already marked with an X—"and here are the two buses." He traced their paths. "You can buy books of bus tickets at any *tabacchi.* Convenience store."

I listened to him intently as I ate, as if he were giving me instructions rather than tips. I had spent the last few months with far too little to do and far too much to think about. Now I looked at the cats on his shirt as I considered my choices: I could go back to bed and lie there looking at the ceiling or I could venture out, following his directions. Dead or alive.

Lying in bed hadn't helped and his excitement was infectious, so I decided I would venture out into the city before my grief settled about me again.

I returned to Lemonland where I could still hear the snoring. I quietly gathered my purse, making sure I put the bus ticket and the map in a safe place. I had my phone. I filled my water bottle and took a granola bar from my suitcase. Lastly I put on my whistle.

It was small and shiny silver with a small ball rolling around inside it. I had bought it at home without telling anyone and had put it on a strong brown leather cord. Russ told me he was sure I would be safe, but he wouldn't be there to pick up the pieces if something went wrong. I had never felt any need for anything like it at home, but my world had tilted on its axis and I generally felt more vulnerable, like a newborn baby thrust into a colder, airier world from what she had known. Then, too, the thought of negotiating this foreign country on my own had added to my fear. I bought the whistle as a kind of vow to myself, that I would protect myself.

I looked up at the picture of Mary. "Wish me luck," I said.

The nuns had seemingly disappeared and even the kitchen sounded quiet. Perhaps they were at their prayers or had gone to church. I resisted the guilt that made me think I should track down the English Church. Cecy had told me at supper the night before that the nuns would buzz us in and out of the electric gates at any time of day until eleven o'clock at night, that once she had to stay out all night because she missed curfew by ten minutes. I wouldn't be gone that long.

I stepped outside into the sunshine. The air was thin and clear, and the sky overhead was a brilliant blue. This time I knew to look for the small electronic button beside the gate, and it was there, and I pushed it. When a voice said, "*Sì?*" I decided to try my Italian name. "Elizabetta Fane," I said, awkwardly. But apparently it was a magic word because the door swung open.

As I began to descend the steep road, stone walls and wrought iron gates beside me, I realized I only had the one ticket, and that if I couldn't find a *tabacchi*, I would have to walk back up these hills. I decided that I would save the ticket and take the bus back.

The map led me down a laneway between yards whose stone fences were topped with shards of broken glass—a message of warning that needed no translation—bright in the early morning sun.

On the edge of the first piazza, I spotted a sign on a tiny store that said *Tabacchi*, and I went inside and purchased two more bus tickets, feeling better equipped and proud of my Italian. As I turned to go, I smiled at the woman standing in line behind me, a woman wrapped in heavy black woolen clothes. She looked at me without smiling back, sucking deeply on her brown cigarette as she reached a gnarled claw of a hand to the young man working behind the counter. I put my bus tickets into my purse, watching as the young man handed her a package of unfiltered cigarettes and a scratch lottery ticket.

I left her to her luck and walked on until suddenly I emerged at a bridge. When I looked down at the river below it and then along its length, I realized that this was the Arno with its well-known succession of bridges.

The water beneath the bridge was like jade, pale green, and at once murky and shining. As I kept walking I moved in shadows on a narrow cobblestone-bricked street that opened into a wide square with an open-air market. With a sense of unreality, I recognized the piazza of Santa Croce. In college my roommate had insisted on watching Regency romance movies and once I thought I was settling in for another one when it turned out to be the far more delightful *A Room with a View.* Santa Croce was *A Room with a View* territory.

I stopped in the market and bought a small oval of fresh soft white cheese—supper at the convent had been a feast, but breakfast had been slim, and I needed more fortification for the day.

As I sat on the church steps and unwrapped my cheese, I thought about the scene in Santa Croce in *A Room with a*

View, the man who was unhappy because of the trouble of the universe, that things didn't fit, the man who could not stop asking *why*. I understood that man.

And then I took a bite of the cheese and found it both mild and tangy at the same time. I looked around me and saw what I imagined was quintessential Italy—old men watching the world go by as they leaned back and smoked; young men standing at counters in suits and colorful leather shoes, throwing back tiny cups of espresso; women arm in arm, wrapped in pashminas—and my calculations changed.

Fifty days had felt like a long time that morning, but seeing Santa Croce made me realize that the time could pass very quickly if I wasted it thinking endlessly about the Everlasting Why.

I hadn't been myself for a few months in my own unhappiness about the trouble of the universe. I had camouflaged my trip as celebration *—I'm turning 50 so I decided to go to Italy for 50 days!*—but now I felt an unexpected ripple of genuine energy and optimism, thinking the way the old Liz thought about things, the Liz before everything fell to pieces, the Liz who made lists and walked with purpose and faced the day with anticipation.

But what did it mean not to waste my time? I certainly wasn't a tourist wanting to see all the sights—I hadn't even made a list of places I wanted to see in Florence. It had been all I could do simply to get myself here. I remembered the astronomer's shirt: at home, I had been mostly dead—lying in bed staring at the ceiling, asking the everlasting why questions. I recalled *A Room with a View* once more, the man's father imploring him to realize, "By the side of the everlasting Why there is a Yes—a transitory Yes if you like, but a Yes."

Maybe that was what Italy was, a box where I could be both dead and alive simultaneously. Maybe I could find even a transitory Yes if I let myself explore, let myself be a bit of a tourist after all.

I tilted my head like Mary once more and unfolded the astronomer's map for ideas of where I might go. I recognized the names of two museums I had heard friends talk about—the Accademia and the Uffizi—and decided those would be good places to start. I figured out the route, gathered my things and my courage, and headed off.

At the corner, signs were affixed to the sides of buildings indicating the road names and the name of the piazza itself. Higher up there were also rectangular silver plates attached to the building and inscribed with numbers. I wondered what they meant.

As I walked, I saw men with what I assumed were cheap designer knock-off purses and art prints displayed on blankets on the ground but I passed them without slowing, remembering the advice of my seatmate on the plane not to even make eye contact with street sellers.

I walked into long first gallery of the Accademia and ahead of me in all his masculine glory under a skylit dome was Florence's most famous resident: Michelangelo's *David.* There was no missing him. I turned to the people near me, so conditioned to comment on what I saw, wanting someone to share the moment with, even just to say, "Wow, it's really the *David*." But no one even met my eye as I walked alone toward him and then around him. It was hard to remember that this was a carving even though at close range I could see tiny chisel marks. There were marble veins and muscles, and determination in his eye. Around me, tourists broke the rules and took photographs.

If Russ were there, he would have researched what was worth seeing in the Accademia, and he would know why scholars thought it was important, how it had been protected during the war, any stories about it. I didn't really know what to look for. Some masterpieces, I knew, were small—the *Mona Lisa*, for instance—and I knew that I could miss seeing great works of art.

But I was alone with the *David*, standing in the milky white February light under a cupola. I made my peace, took a deep breath, and settled into myself and the light.

I began to enjoy the freedom of moving alone through the galleries, going past art that did not speak to me, that did not invite me to gaze longer, returning to the art I liked, lingering. The effect was meditative.

Eventually I came back to the *David* and wondered what the female equivalent would be, the idealized woman. The best I could think of was the *Venus de Milo*, whose arms had been broken off. The thought didn't feel terribly encouraging.

What most captured my imagination was a series of large, heavy, rough sculptures, figures emerging from stone that turned out to be Michelangelo's work too. That was how I felt, half-done, undone, still emerging. I wondered whether these statues had been deliberately left undone or if they'd been discarded because of some flaw in the stone or some commissioned work or even the sculptor's old age. I sat down on an austere wooden bench to read the little English card next to one of the displays, but when I saw that they were called the Prisoners or Slaves, it raised even more questions for me.

It felt awfully good to sit, and I realized that my energy was flagging, still jet-lagged. As I sat, a woman holding up a stick with a tennis ball dangling from the end headed toward the sculptures, like a parade marshal with an upraised baton in the Oktoberfest parade back home. In her wake a group of tourists followed. The guide began to gesture with her hands as she explained in English that the sculptures had been deliberately left unfinished, carved from marble to represent people bound by the earth, the struggle to free the spirit from matter. A man asked a question and the guide turned toward him to answer so I couldn't hear her reply and realized I probably shouldn't be eavesdropping anyhow. As they traipsed off, it occurred to me that, though they looked like a family of ducklings waddling along, these tourists were getting their questions answered.

Was I finding answers to my questions? It wasn't as simple as that. It was more like when I was very pregnant with Timothy and the midwife told me he had dropped. I had struggled to breathe deeply in late pregnancy as he pressed up against my lungs. I didn't know what it meant for a baby to drop into position to be ready to be born but I did know I could finally breathe more fully. That was what the morning at the museum had been, a bit more freedom to breathe.

In my energy of the morning, I had imagined I could do two museums in one day but now jet lag decided otherwise. It had been good to get out of my own head and to be a tourist but I had seen enough for one day—I would not tempt Stendahl syndrome by subjecting myself to too much art. Perhaps on another day I would join a tour for my visit to the Uffizi. Before I left the Accademia, I swallowed my pride and stopped in the gift shop to buy a tourist guide to Florence.

As I walked back toward the bridge where I could catch the bus, I traversed narrow streets not always well marked at intersections, although there were a variety of the silver signs with the numbers 1966 on them. Was it a date? In a city that was hundreds of years old, I wondered what twentieth-century event had been important enough to mark. I did not know. I also gradually became aware that I must have taken a wrong turn somewhere. Suddenly, I found myself standing in the shade of an enormous building.

The Duomo. I had seen its famous red-brick domed roof from the taxi, but up close I could see that the iconic building itself was covered with white, red, and green marble, in an almost dizzying pattern. The square around the Duomo was filled with more people than Santa Croce had held, many of them stopping and staring as I was, or taking pictures of this gigantic structure that seemed to appear out of nowhere.

There were lineups to climb the Duomo but the doors to the building were open on the sides. As I walked in, I remembered that it was a church, although I couldn't imagine anyone worshipping there. I looked up at the inside of the dome, at the massive ceiling, covered with paintings. My neck was still tight from the plane ride, and I wanted to sit down, but when I looked, the church itself had no pews, no chairs. It was as cavernous as an airplane hangar. I estimated it to be as long as two or three city blocks. It was almost too big to take in, and grander than anything I had ever seen before.

I leaned against a wall and looked up again at the inside of the dome. I thought of the story I'd heard years before about how the Duomo had been built without a roof, in faith that someday someone would figure out how to build a dome on top of it. Clearly they had. There was something fortifying about that for me, saying that a question implied an answer even if you had wait centuries for it.

The domed ceiling was painted in bright colors with scenes I assumed were from the Bible, but they looked like a jumble of figures as foreign to me as the Italian language. I began to feel shaky with fatigue and strangeness and grief, more dead than alive, as though someone was pushing the air out of my lungs once more. I pulled out the astronomer's map and decided I didn't care if I looked like a tourist: I would keep the map out and check it at each turn so I could get back to the bridge.

I successfully found my way onto the bus that circled its way up the hill although I got off a stop too soon and had to walk the last streets to the convent. I breathed a sigh of relief when the gate clanged shut behind me.

The convent still seemed silent and empty, although someone was evidently there to open the gate. As I entered the stone building, I became aware of how strange it was what you could and couldn't hear. I could hear my own footsteps, and they sounded loud on the marble, but there weren't the aches and creaks of an old wooden house or the typical sounds of plumbing or heating systems. Nor were there sounds from outside. That morning I had heard voices and sounds as I came around the corner that led from the walkway, but those sounds didn't seem to bend around corners. Now they were absent altogether. It was a question of echoes. It was the echoes that had stopped.

When I opened the door to the Lemonland apartment, Honey was stretched out on the long orange couch in the common room, typing on her phone.

"Hey there," she said, bending her legs so there was space for me on the couch. She tapped one of her feet in invitation for me to sit. "Cecy said to say bye. Where did you go?"

I was more than happy to sit. I told her about the Accademia. "Have you been?"

She wrinkled her nose. "My folks took me to so many museums when I was little that I'm kind of allergic to them now."

"You sound like my kids," I said.

"You have kids?"

Did I have kids? It was the most essential thing about me. I pulled out my own phone and found pictures.

"They're super cute," she said. Then she pointed at Russ. "And that's your guy?"

I nodded and settled back into the couch. It was very comfortable. "Where are the nuns?"

"It's their day out," she said. "They'll be back in an hour or so. Want to explore a bit?"

My feet said no, but my brain said that I would rather explore while the nuns weren't there than when they were. "Sure," I said. "Let me put my stuff away first."

I walked back into my room. The Virgin Mary looked over at me. "I made it back," I said to the painting, and somehow it smiled beatifically at me.

What I most wanted to see was their chapel. Honey had told me the nuns said we were always welcome to join their services, but I wanted to know what I would be getting myself into before I just walked in. We went down the marble staircase and toward the back of the building.

The chapel was a long narrow room with wooden benches and kneelers on either side. Behind the altar was a dazzling, explosion of a gold cross and Jesus hanging upon it. I had heard it said that the difference between Catholic and Protestant churches was that in the Catholic church, Jesus hangs on the cross while Protestant churches have empty crosses. This chapel felt a bit like a museum, beautiful but also somehow preserved. I looked at the figure on the cross. Was this Italian Jesus the same as the Jesus I knew?

We were walking back across the walkway to our apartment when we heard the nuns returning and stopped to watch. I hadn't realized there were quite so many of them. There were probably eighteen nuns, most of them elderly but several my age or younger. They arrived chattering, and for some reason I thought of the children's books about Madeline where the class of girls walked in two straight lines. Maybe this *was* a boarding school. The *suore* didn't walk in straight lines but they did walk in pairs. The beetle-browed nun stalked past without looking up but the little nun with the big eyes, Salvia, waved up at us. There was something relaxed and almost windblown about them.

"Where do you think they went?" I asked Honey.

"Cecy asked them that once," she said. "They apparently have an annual pass to the Pinocchio Park so they go there every Sunday after Mass."

"The *what*?"

"Right? That's what I said. They say we can join them any Sunday afternoon if we want."

Was there really such a thing as a Pinocchio Park? Was it possible that in a city of countless treasures and stunning beauty, a city that people escaped to, that sometimes what you had to do was escape *from* it, to go to a shopping mall or a theme park?

10

THE SIMPLE WAY MY HUSBAND AND SONS PUT IT WAS that I was having an adventure—*un'avventura*, as my six weeks of Italian classes had taught me to say. I heard one of the boys say it to a friend: Mom loves gardening now and she's going on a gardening adventure to Italy.

They weren't wrong. It was another true way of telling the story.

When everything fell apart this past October and I took a leave from my job, I needed something to do, something simple, somewhere I could make a difference, somewhere real. I also needed something that would tire me out and help me fall instantly asleep when I dropped into bed at night, instead of staring at the ceiling and rehashing it all. I decided I would clean the house. I had said for years that our house needed a good spring cleaning—no, that was not strictly true. What I'd said was that the house had never been as clean as it was when I was eight-and-a-half months pregnant, and nesting, that what my house needed was for me to have another baby. I had joked that I should bring a pregnant woman home to capture that nesting power, like a turbine converting wind or water into energy.

So, at the end of October, I scrubbed floors and cleaned out drawers as well as I ever had while nesting.

But to my disappointment, it turned out my house was not as dirty as I'd thought and within a week I had turned the house into a shining palace of order a 1950s housewife would have envied.

The next day, I woke up slightly panicked about how I would fill the hours until I could fall asleep again. I knew I didn't want to go out for lunch with friends and that I wasn't ready to return to work. While I waited for the coffee to drip through the machine, I looked out the window to where the morning glories twined their way up the garage wall. They had been full with brilliant blue flowers every day that fall, one bright spot of beauty, but this morning the leaves dangled limp and withered as with sudden shock. I looked out at the lawn and it was covered with a heavy frost.

"The garden," I said aloud to myself, and it felt like an unexpected answer to a riddle. I had never really gardened, unlike many of my neighbors who knew the names of plants, and who said words like *soil amendment*, *acidity*, and *alkalinity*, while I just nodded, smiled, and pretended those words had meaning to me. We had a garden, of course, because we live in suburbia and that's what you do. It had always been what I called low maintenance, which mostly meant that we forgot to cut down whatever we'd planted in the spring, leaving snow to cover our sins of omission, forgotten flowers easily dug under again the following spring as we quickly stuck in cheerfully colorful replacements from the garden center.

Last fall had been different. I had not torn my clothes and poured ashes on my head after it happened but starting that morning and all through November, I hacked away at the garden, and poured compost and manure over it. What I did might be called gardening, but in my mind I called it anti-gardening—ripping and pulling vines, sawing away at peony bushes, tearing at withered day lilies. It was incredibly satisfying. When Eva told me about the convent and the olive groves, I had been willing to work in the gardens, but it was the thought of anti-gardening on a bigger scale that appealed to me.

Then, for Christmas, Russ gave me a subscription to a gardening magazine and a new pair of secateurs, as if gardening was the hobby I'd chosen to fill my empty nest—and I thought half-seriously about taking a swipe at him with the shears.

11

On the first Monday morning at the convent—*lunedì mattina*—I pulled on the jeans I had worn all November when I was anti-gardening and they felt looser than they had when I last wore them. I added a fleece jacket and the boots I had brought. *I can at least look the part,* I thought.

Honey joined me for breakfast, a bandanna around her hair, her eyes still half asleep. She poured coffee into her mug and drank it black, to the dismay of the nun who watched her, and then filled her cup again. I realized that when Honey had passed on Cecy's goodbye, it meant that Cecy had left for good. I couldn't say I would miss her.

As we finished our breakfast, the little nun, Salvia, who was apparently the only one who spoke English, came into the dining room. She took the basket of bread from our table and shyly gestured to signal to Honey and to me to follow her out to the terrace.

It was chilly but dazzling early morning sunlight. Salvia opened a small wooden cupboard-like door built into the low stone wall surrounding the terrace and took out a metal oil can. She passed the basket around, offering bread to us. I didn't think we could refuse so I took a slice as though it was a very large piece of communion bread. Then, in the early morning light, she poured olive oil over the bread we held.

"This," she said. "Here we produce this. It is good to know what it will be before you start. *Mangia*," she said, and we did. I could tell from Honey's face that this hadn't been part of her experience before either. The oil was green and fresh and peppery, all the things Eva's oil had been, with the added benefit of being served in the Italian sunshine instead of indoors in winter on the far side of the world.

My hands were covered in olive oil but I rubbed them together, letting the oil make my hands soft and ready.

"To prune the trees it takes five weeks," she explained. "If we have no rain. We plant the gardens when the frost is no more."

As we ate, an elderly man came out of the convent carrying a box of medieval-looking implements. From his clothes—a long, brown habit tied at the waist with rope—it was clear he was a monk. When he kissed Salvia on both cheeks, I was glad Cecy had left so I didn't have to hear her commentary.

"This is *Fra* Niccolò," Salvia said by way of introduction, and Niccolò gave quick bows of his head to each of us. I felt an urge to curtsy, but I suppressed it. "You know Miele. This is Elizabetta. She is just arrived." A second time he bowed his head to me and this time I bowed mine in return. "Each year Niccolò come to help the pruning of the trees and to deliver the olives for the pressing."

"Good morning," he said in careful, accented English.

Niccolò was tall and vigorous, but I suspected he was over sixty and possibly over seventy. With shaky hands he poured green olive oil from Salvia's jug into a small shot glass he took from somewhere in his robe. He drank it down and then raised an arm to the true-blue sky and swept his hand across the grove of trees with a nod of his head. He smacked his lips, returned his glass to the intricate secret recesses of his robe, and handed the oil back to Salvia. She put the oil can into the cupboard door in the wall and closed it. Then she gave us a wave, wished us a good morning, and left us to return into the house.

"*Allora*," Niccolò said, handing each of us a small hatchet before shouldering his own. Mine was lighter than I expected.

"This is my forty-seven year tending the olives. *Se Dio vuole*, I will have fifty years. We begin?"

We followed him, guessing at some of his Italian words, descending into the early morning shadows of the olive grove where the grass was wet and cold.

Niccolò looked at a small slip of a tree and shook his head. He found another tree that was large and lush and full, and lifted his hatchet and began hacking away at the branches in the center of the tree. His movements looked violent and almost haphazard. I had to stamp my feet to keep them warm as he cut away at the tree while we watched. Twenty minutes later, he had cleaned out the entire lower center of the tree, while leaving the outer branches virtually untouched.

I hated to say it, but the tree had looked far better and healthier before he started. Cautiously I told him so and asked the reason for the extreme pruning.

"No oil from a beautiful tree," he said, chopping away at the remaining small branches that had grown out of the main trunk.

It reminded me of the time I had tried to take a pottery class. I could never understand when my work was good and when it was not. I'd been to pottery sales before and other than the ones where the glazes were clearly uneven or there were cracks or pieces missing, I couldn't tell a good piece of pottery from a poor one. My instructor said that my pots were uneven, that one side was thinner than another, but I honestly couldn't see this or feel it with my hands. It was like that in the olive grove—I watched as Niccolò pruned the tree, and I was confused by which branches were cut off and which were left. I had quit my pottery class. I hoped I could do better at pruning.

Niccolò moved on to the next tree, which was gnarled and ancient and taller than the first one. There was a small stepladder under this tree. He handed Honey his hatchet while he mounted the stool and climbed into the branches in the center of the tree. I held my breath as he rose.

Before taking his hatchet back from Honey, he turned as if on a stage, to face us, his audience of two. "You hack an old tree. Is very good," he said, making a chopping motion with his right hand as if to remove his left arm at the inner elbow. "He will crescendo again from the energy in the roots and trunk. A young tree will not.

"He requires *ferite greggie*—the large, egregious wounds—to grow the fruit. If not—" Here he waved his fingers as if making jazz hands—"he becomes chaos."

I didn't even know what the word "egregious" meant but there was something satisfying about saying the words under my breath—*large, egregious wounds*.

We were to walk up to a perfectly healthy, lush, full olive tree and slash away at it until it looked spindly and bare. The important thing, Niccolò told us, was getting light to the center of the tree, lopping off all the vigorous young shoots that filled its core, only leaving a few to grow. The energy of the tree could then go into producing olives rather than leaves. "A bird, he can fly through the center of a well-pruned olive tree," he explained.

It was not what I'd expected but it felt even more satisfying than my anti-gardening at home. Still, at first, I was over-cautious. Niccolò had to call me back three times to my first tree. "Good to be careful," he said. "This tree is probably five hundred years old, and you no want to kill him, but he can accept the pruning."

His words fell into a deep place in me, like olive oil finding every hole in a piece of bread, saturating it. He meant the trees. Of course he did. It was I who read into his words.

I thought of my friend Joanna. When she was divorced, when her husband left her, she was commuting to Toronto for work. She used to get stuck in rush-hour traffic and would find herself trying to discover meaning and messages in the billboard signs flashing around her. Eventually she went to therapy and now we could even laugh about it, sending each other screenshots of billboards we passed, explaining what we might do if we took them as directives. I wondered what she would think of the Florentine signs advertising strippers and alcohol.

But it wasn't hard to do the same thing in the olive grove, to see it all as pure metaphor, as promise, as hope that maybe I could find my way back to my life again, that I could find a Yes by the side of the Everlasting Why. It felt patently obvious to me—it wasn't a stretch at all—that sometimes an olive tree was more than an olive tree.

We pruned five trees that first morning, including the first one Niccolò had done. I thought of the summer Tim had spent tree-planting in northern Ontario, how he was paid per tree. It was good we didn't have a quota.

I was glad and much warmer by the time we stopped for lunch. Niccolò explained we would have a couple of hours off after lunch to rest. I assumed that the rest was for him but when I got up from the table after eating bean soup and something somewhat like pizza, I felt the double ache of jet lag and physical labor in my body and was glad to lie on my bed as I had done as a child during rest period at camp. There was a sunbeam on my bed, warming me, and my eyes grew heavy.

When Honey knocked on my door an hour later, I had no idea what time it was or even where I was, but I dragged myself up, nonetheless. I looked up at the portrait of Mary. "You want to take my shift this afternoon?" Her enigmatic half-smile did not say yes, so I put my boots back on.

The afternoon work was shorter and had a different rhythm. Niccolò unfolded a large brown tarpaulin on the grass. We were to put the branches we'd cut that morning on it and drag it to a large, bricked depression in the ground, far from the olive grove, where we were to throw the branches in. Niccolò stood at the edge of the pit, retrieving larger limbs he said the monks would use to carve into wooden utensils to sell to tourists.

"*Stai attenta*, Elizabetta," he said to me, holding up a cautioning finger. "No let the branches get close to the *glicine*."

"The *glicine*?" I asked, confused. The word reminded me of the French word for pool—*piscine*—and there were none of those in evidence.

Niccolò walked over to the wall nearby and gently touched a gnarled *glicine* branch. "He is a thousand years old. He is *magnifico*." The branch stretched out along the entire length of the stone wall, but it looked like one of the wiry old men I had seen in the Santa Croce piazza, ash hanging perilously off the end of his cigarette, sitting back like he had all the time in the world, as if he would inhale eventually but for now would relax in the sun and watch the world go by.

But I understood what Niccolò meant. He didn't want any olive branches touching anywhere near the plant for fear of burning it down when the branches were burned. Even if the *glicine* was ugly, it was impressive in its age and size. I had been impressed that Niccolò had worked this olive grove for forty-seven years, but the five-hundred-year-old olive tree and the thousand-year-old *glicine* made him seem almost as much of a newcomer as me. The backs of my thighs ached as I bent to gather the branches and leaves that had fallen outside the pit and to sweep them inside it. Niccolò nodded approval.

When we had finished gathering the day's branches, Niccolò oiled our hatchets with what he described dismissively as poor-quality olive oil. This would keep them sharp and ready for the next day.

I'm pruning metaphorical trees, I texted Russ that evening after another gourmet supper—this time arugula salad, veal and risotto, an olive oil cake, and more cheese—typing with only my left hand as my right hand was too sore. *Which doesn't explain the blisters.*

12

LAST FALL, I FREQUENTLY THOUGHT OF *The Velveteen Rabbit*. I had long savored the story of the stuffed rabbit who was loved so well that his fur became shabby and worn. *The Velveteen Rabbit* told me that once you had been made real by love you could never be unreal again. From my first reading, I knew this was not a children's book at all, but a book for adults.

Everyone had a different story about how love made them real, but I found it in the muscle memory of my stomach. Before I had the boys, my stomach was slightly concave, but afterwards, although I'd lost all the baby weight easily, my stomach always protruded just a little, like elastic that had been stretched until it was unable to return to its original shape. I recognized that a child creates his own space where there was no space before, and that this stretching had grounded me, made me real.

Last fall, though, the comfort I took in this story evaporated as I thought of myself as being like the same stuffed rabbit, now tossed on the ash heap. I went searching for the book and found it in Jackson's closet. I sat on his bed and found that part of the book:

He thought of those long sunlit hours in the garden—how happy they were—and a great sadness came over him. He seemed to see them all pass before him, each more beautiful than the other. Of what use was it to be loved only to lose one's beauty and become Real if it all ended like this?

"Exactly," I said in a shaky voice before I burst into tears, knowing that no one was home to hear me.

I read more and even the sense of shared sadness left me when a fairy came and transformed the rabbit and gave him real hind legs. No fairy was going to rescue me. Mothers were to rescue themselves, were supposed to retire from parenting, to slow down, to bask in the glory of a job well done. They were supposed to adapt to the change of seasons with maturity, to accept that all good things come to an end.

And perhaps I could have done all this if it had only been the empty nest. I could have adopted another cat or taken up a new hobby as the rummage sale book had suggested. I could have thrown myself into my work where my parenting skills were an asset, where I could be the mother duck of my organization.

But this felt like an end to motherhood in all the parts of my life. It was not simply a feeling of nostalgia or obsolescence, a sense of not being needed. It was far worse than that: it was not being wanted. Not being welcome. Having lost the right to know my children's hearts, the right to share my own heart.

Large egregious wounds.

13

Like cat stretch to downward dog, like inhale and exhale, like high tide to low tide, the nuns moved seamlessly from prayer to work to prayer again. Salvia explained shyly one afternoon that she and several of the other nuns taught children at a nearby school every morning. I wondered whether they walked to the school in pairs, but it turned out they drove there in the convent's van.

I was not a nun, as I had told my airplane seatmate—had he made it to Abu Dhabi?—and so my movement was from work to food to bed to work, at least for the first few days. At home, I felt religious because I went to church on Sunday mornings. Here I felt positively pagan. And ravenous.

The rhythm of the convent found us eating in the dark of a late winter morning, gathering our tools and beginning our work as the sky began to lighten around us. Often one of the older *suore* would refill our water bottles midmorning or sometimes on cold days would bring coffee and hot milk, speaking to us in Italian with words that had an encouraging tone although we had no idea what she was saying. We finished our work just after noon, ate lunch, and then went to our rooms to nap while the nuns went to their prayers.

Napping didn't feel decadent either, although it did feel like a blessing to be able to unwind and be perfectly still. My father had always said that fresh air gave the best appetite and that was certainly true, but now it also gave me the best sleep I'd ever had. I'd always been a terrible sleeper; now I slept like one of the small green lizards we saw dozing in the sunshine on the convent terrace walls on warmer afternoons, and I woke up more refreshed from a one-hour nap than I ever imagined possible.

After our short afternoon shift, we had another few hours to ourselves before supper. The tiny library on the table in our common room contained a total of four English books: two about geology, one a theology text, and the last a science fiction novel. I also had my new tourist guide. The second day of work, I tried to read the theology book, but it was hard to follow, and I was weary. I could download a book but I didn't actually want to read. Homesickness and heavy thoughts of the Everlasting Why set in as the sun lowered itself in the sky. I sat on the chair in the common room and signed myself up for a tour the following Saturday afternoon, seeking a transitory Yes—or at least something to fill the hours. Honey lay on the orange couch watching television. We tried to guess at the plot of what we thought was probably an Italian soap opera.

The next day, I decided to use the time to email my family:

Buongiorno! Come sta? Sta bene. Are you impressed with my Italian? I hope you are all doing well and not missing me TOO much. You wouldn't believe the place I'm staying at. It's stunning. Good food and fantastic place. Only one of the nuns speaks English but between her and the Italian classes I did at home, I'm doing well on my adventure. There's another woman staying here too and we're about a dozen trees into what I estimate to be about 150. Other than the blisters and sore muscles, no mishaps. Write soon. I miss you. Love, Mom

It felt as though I was writing in a foreign tongue, in Mom language. It made me think of *The Princess Bride* and how the princess realized that when Westley said, "As you wish," what he really meant was "I love you." If I could translate my breezy email into the language of my heart, it would be closer to the groans of labor pains. It would say: there's half a world between us and once we were connected and you resided right inside me, and I love you fiercely beyond these words I'm using to try to narrow the space between us, to build a bridge back to the place where our hearts beat next to one another.

But that was not something they could hear from me. My job was to put my own feelings and needs aside, to be The Mother and to tend to them as I always did, even though now there was more than an ocean between us with the events that had changed everything. There was also no possibility of saying the rest of what I needed to say to them, even in code. Then, too, I felt we had oddly shifted roles: where I had always been the safe landing spot, home, for my children, now I was the one who had been launched out of my safe cocoon into a bigger world, sending reports back home to them.

I didn't know what else I should do with this chunk of the afternoon when jet lag and homesickness hit: there wasn't enough time to go to a museum, and I wasn't keen on being out after dark either. I sat in the chair beside the couch where Honey lay and looked idly through my guidebook.

"Have you been to the Piazzale Michelangelo?" I asked her. "The book says it's the best view of Florence, and I think it's not too far from here."

"It is a good view," she said. "But it's uphill on the way back. I saw the sunset from there when all we were doing was washing bottles. I'm too tired to do it now that we're lumberjacking."

I was tired myself, but I found myself returning to the astronomer and his cat shirt. If I sat on the couch in this lonesome hour, I knew it would be a choice of death. I decided I would give life a try once more. I took a quick shower and slipped my whistle under my clothes. I looked up at Mary. "I'm safe, aren't I?" I asked. "This isn't the part of the movie where the scary music starts, is it?"

I had read extensively about solo women travelers when I was deciding whether to come to Florence on my own, when

I felt vulnerable, anxiety moving through my belly like a contraction every time I thought about my trip. Everything said that Florence was safe for women travelers, that the main risk was pickpockets, but nonetheless I had found myself filled with images of being lost in a suburban maze, being groped on a bus, or being dragged into bushes.

I decided to stick to roads, rather than to take the laneways I had followed on my first day. Although cars whizzed past me at a rate that meant they would likely be unable to even see any need for help let alone stop, I was glad that there were no bushes on my route, only towering, leafless trees with colorful peeling bark forming a canopy over the sidewalk and the road.

I came to the same piazza where I had bought the bus tickets and was proud of myself for recognizing it. I also noticed the same old woman who had bought the lottery ticket. She was again wrapped in her heavy, black woolens and smoking a cigarette in the shadow of the building. As I crossed the piazza, this time going in the opposite direction from the Arno, I watched her look at the cigarette as if questioning how quickly it had burned down, then drop it to the ground, grind it under an ancient small black leather boot that emerged from her dark layers, and then retreat inside.

After only a fifteen-minute walk, I saw the Piazzale Michelangelo on the other side of the road. I waited a full five minutes for a break in the traffic and then dashed across the road.

It was the iconic postcard view of Florence: gazing back at the city, I could see the bridges crossing the Arno, the Duomo at eye level, and above that the hills to the north of the city. The sun had moved lower into the sky, the transparent light of a late winter afternoon, even though it was warm enough that I only needed to wear a fleece jacket. I was not alone in the piazza. There were small clusters of tourists, many of them sitting on the stairs, waiting for the sunset that was about an hour and a half away. Many of them wore a black smudge on their foreheads. I wondered at it—I hadn't noticed anyone else with that kind of mark since arriving in Florence.

In the wide piazza were a dozen idling taxis and buses spewing exhaust, but in the center of them stood a replica of the *David*. There were also more of the men hawking purses and da Vinci prints. I walked the full length of the rail overlooking the city, stopping only when several couples asked me to take their photos. Just before I took a second photo, I noticed a church higher up the hill, significantly higher. I decided to see what the view was like from there before I returned to the convent.

After risking my life again crossing the busy road, I began the ascent. There were stairs and stairs and stairs leading up to the church, joining together from one side and another, as if I were scaling a waterfall with little outcroppings of rock as landings. As the sound of my breathing increased in my ears, I noticed a corresponding lessening of the sound of the traffic below. I could see the church ahead of me, one more steep flight of steps up. The face of the church, like the Duomo, was covered in a white, green, and red marble façade—*was there anything in Italy that wasn't red, white, and green?*—but the rest of the church was old, undecorated stone. I turned and looked around at the panorama below me. It was breathtaking even for someone whose breath had already been taken by the climb.

Just below me, I watched two elderly nuns in black make their way slowly up the stairs, arm in arm. Like the tourists in the Piazzale Michelangelo, they both wore black marks on their foreheads, marks I now realized were crosses. They did not pause as I had but opened a door in the façade of the church and went inside. When a couple of tourists stepped out the same door, I decided to go in.

I was struck first by the chill of the church. It was shadowed and as cold as ice water. It was also big, although very different from the Duomo. Rather than being like an enormous airplane hangar, this church felt like being inside a ship, wooden ribs visible on the roof and sides. I walked around the edge and smelled ancient smells, damp stone and incense, feeling like a stranger in this church.

I was a lifelong Baptist, and the extent of my ecumenism before this trip had been attending a baptism in an ornate Eastern Orthodox church, once visiting a Catholic church, and attending a bat mitzvah celebration in the gym of a synagogue as well as speaking in various church basements about the work my organization did. I wasn't afraid about any of the Italian churches, but I felt much like I did about speaking Italian, uncertain how to enter in.

I tried to seek recognition among the symbols carved into pillars, embedded in floor tiles, statues, and artwork as I walked about the church. I had climbed to the top of the church when I heard it begin. Men's voices chanted, singing, their voices filling the spaces. It took me a few minutes to realize the music wasn't coming from someone's phone or a speaker system.

I followed the sound down to the main level, and then to the back interior of the church where a small flight of stairs must have been cut deep into the hillside. At the bottom of those steps, hidden behind a wall of wrought iron bars more like a bird cage than a prison, a group of monks stood in a semicircle against the walls. They wore identical white robes, and they sang a song that lifted into the ceiling that was vaulted in high arches, half-lit by flickering lanterns within the enclosed area, half-shadowed. *Chiaroscuro*, my guidebook said of this kind of light.

I stayed at the back, leaning against one of the tall cold marble pillars. Ahead of me were rows of wooden benches with kneelers in front of each row. There were five people kneeling, including the two nuns I had earlier seen come into the church.

What spoke to me were the silences and the unisons, eight voices singing as one, strengthening as they sang together. There was a melancholy quality to it that struck me as faithful. This was not a performance but a ritual.

Ritual. I turned the word over on my tongue as I had done with Italian words. Ritual was as foreign to my experience as Italian was. There was something ancient and still in this music. I strained to understand the words and could understand nothing. I had no idea whether it was Italian or Latin. It reminded me of the time long ago when I'd been at the ballet with my aunt and was transported by the grace of arms and legs, oblivious to the story if there even was one.

One monk would start a line of music and then there would be a note slightly lower than the rest and then a brief pause and the others would join in. They were replying to one another, a kind of grace in the silences between their singing, surrounding it.

I looked at the faces of the monks and they looked very much like the faces on the plaster busts in the Accademia. Several of these monks were old but not all of them. Like the tourists and the nuns, they wore black crosses on their foreheads. One monk caught my attention. He was tall, lanky, and spectacled. He was middle-aged and wore Birkenstocks beneath his robe. He reminded me of the husband of a teacher I had babysat for when I was a teenager. When he came out of the enclosure to offer communion wafers, it didn't feel respectful to join in when I didn't know what they were saying, so I stayed in my seat.

But I felt still inside and had a sense that this was a place I could return to.

Later that evening, after I returned safely to the convent and ate another glorious meal—this time featuring a hearty bean soup piled with Parmesan, with pomegranates and more cheese after the meal—I looked online to try to learn more about the forehead smudges and the church. The crosses were for Ash Wednesday, and the church was called San Miniato, and, like the *glicine*, it was a thousand years old. The service I had stumbled into was called the Vespers Mass and it happened each day at the end of day and was open to the public. Vespers was the equivalent to the song we sang at the overnight camp I went to when I was a child: *Day is done, gone the sun, from the lake, from the hills, from the sky. All is well, safely rest: God is nigh.*

14

When I gave my resignation at the board meeting at the end of October last year, I could not speak of why I was leaving other than to say it was a personal matter that was going to require my time and attention.

That day I went home and saw the pumpkin I'd bought at the farmers' market sitting on our kitchen counter. It had long been a family tradition to carve pumpkins together, Russ and I doing most of the scooping out of the pumpkin guts, and the boys doing the design and carving.

An hour later Russ came home and found me sitting alone in tears on the back porch, carving a face into the lone pumpkin so we would have something festive to put out for Halloween.

The next day I was sorting through my files and packing up my personal belongings when Peg knocked on my office door and came in, shutting the door behind her.

Peg was a retired doctor and one of my staunchest allies on the board of directors. She had a craggy face, short gray hair, and a blunt manner. She seated herself in the chair where so many volunteers, staff, and clients had sat, waiting for me to dispense my wisdom. Peg didn't wait.

"Are you well, lass?" she asked.

I had already taken a leave of absence, barely slept, ached with grief as I had when my father died, and couldn't concentrate on my work. I had cried myself to sleep for the last few weeks, learning to cry silently and without moving. But she was asking more whether I had been diagnosed with cancer or a heart condition.

"I'm not sick," I said.

"I got to thinking last night that, if you were, you should take a longer leave instead of resigning," she said. "It's none of my business to know, but I wanted to make sure we weren't steering you wrong."

My eyes welled up at her caring. "Other than the joys of menopause," I said, "I'm healthy. Thanks." I couldn't tell her what actually ailed me. Not yet.

I thought back to last summer. I had called it The Flood because it lasted a month. If it lasted forty full days, I told myself, I would regret not having built myself an ark. After three weeks of my never-ending period, I went to the doctor and she had just shrugged her thirty-year-old shoulders, saying that at my age and stage of life, anything was possible, that there was no normal. "Some women sail through menopause," she said. "You can hope this isn't too long for you." She explained what to do if I began hemorrhaging and put me on iron tablets, but she was largely unconcerned.

"That's not an easy time either," Peg said. "I had patient after patient go through the change and no two of them alike. Then it was my turn, and nothing I knew prepared me for it. But menopause wasn't the end of me either, although at times I thought it could be."

After she left, I took down the artwork in my office. I had on the wall a painting my friend Joanna had given me the year Tim left home. It was of an open milkweed pod with seeds taking flight. Beneath the pod was a quote from a poem by Mary Oliver that reminded me that there was a time to let go of even the things we held tight against our bones.

October was the time for plants to let go of their seeds, to send them out into the air. The plant could only release the seeds, not control where they went. The seeds would land where the wind would take them. New life would spring up from those seeds even though the plant itself might look as if it was dying.

I was terrified all of this might be the end of me.

15

I HAD FOUND A TOUR COMPANY CALLED *La Dolce Vita* and signed myself up for a tour of the Uffizi on Saturday afternoon. I asked Honey if she wanted to join me—*look at me, being a tourist, choosing life*—but although she didn't have other plans, she still resisted the idea of going to a museum. She thought she might go out with a running group she'd joined when she had first arrived in Florence.

According to my guidebook, the Uffizi was reportedly the place where Stendahl and countless others had become distraught and overwhelmed by the surfeit of art that was utterly different from natural beauty. Natural beauty could inspire awe and even terror but the abundance of art and design in Italy was a different kind of overwhelming altogether. I thought about it as I walked to the museum, past colorful stuccoed houses with ornate iron scrollwork over every window, and past carvings on the sides of buildings. Everything about Italy pushed against the cookie-cutter utilitarian design of malls and houses back at home.

Early to the tour, I walked around the courtyard outside the Uffizi, which was surrounded by elevated statues of figures from Italian history. Our guide had said she would meet us under the statue of Lorenzo il Magnifico. It was the same word Niccolò had used to describe the spreading plant in the convent gardens. I wondered whether this figure would have any resemblance to the gnarled branches of the *glicine*.

As I looked for Lorenzo, I saw a statue of Dante, finger to his chin as if pondering. His stern face made me think about how he had never been allowed back in the city I now stood in. Under my breath I repeated his words, words I had come to know well: "Midway on life's journey I found myself alone in a dark wood where the right way was lost." So far, other than the one wrong turn, I had not really been lost in Florence, had seemingly not been followed. But still I wore my whistle under my clothes each time I left the convent.

I kept looking for the statue of Lorenzo. There were so many statues and carvings, even in this small area, and I hadn't even gone inside the museum yet—I was glad I had opted for a tour instead of trying to negotiate its splendors on my own.

By the time I found Lorenzo, our guide was standing beneath him as she had said she would be. She carried a peacock feather in place of the other guide's tennis ball on a stick. This guide was a heavy-set, middle-aged woman dressed entirely in black like a dancer, a black jersey dress and black sandals with severely bobbed jet-black hair and thick square glasses, her lips a slash of red.

I heard my name being called off the list of tour members, the Italian way: Elizabetta. I didn't say what I always said—*it's Liz*—instead letting the Italian syllables settle over me like one of the pashminas for sale in the little street stalls I had passed in the piazza outside the Uffizi. I raised my hand with a smile.

"*Allora . . .*" I heard our leader say. *Allora.* I often heard the nuns and Niccolò say the word. I had looked it up. That's what the tour leader said before she introduced herself. *Allora,* let's begin.

Before we entered, she explained to us that Lorenzo il Magnifico had been one of the Medici, the leading family of Florence, who had made the city into one of art. She showed us the raised corridor the Medici had taken to get to their offices—their *uffizi*—high above the plague-ridden hordes of average Florentines. She told us how much art was reposited in the edifice built in a U-shape; she told us of the bombing of the Uffizi thirty years before and cautioned us to leave behind anything that might cause concern to the security guards. Finally she told us of Stendahl syndrome.

"We're only going to scratch the surface today," she said. "You could spend a year at the Uffizi just studying the ceilings and floors. It can be overwhelming. Every day, there's always two or three people who have to receive medical attention or who leave the museum sobbing in exhaustion. So we choose selectively and you see the best of the best."

We set off, a group of twenty-five, nineteen of whom were women, like a flock of sheep following the blue feather. We passed at least a hundred people lining up for general admission—this was the most tourist-dense area I had been to yet—and saw another group whose leader carried a hot pink feather leader and another with a closed plaid umbrella serving the same function. I noticed women significantly outnumbered men here: they all looked like they belonged to book clubs that had read *Under the Tuscan Sun* and were here to try their chances at a muscular poet and a villa of their own. I followed our leader as we passed guards brandishing wands and through gates and metal detectors—there was more security here than at Florence's airport—and waited as three members of our group left their cameras with security.

As we traipsed behind the peacock feather up four flights of winding marble stairs, I felt the pruning of trees and the climb to San Miniato in my legs. We passed another security checkpoint and entered a long, vast corridor. The floor of inlaid mosaics caught my eye, and then I looked along the windows, punctuated here and there with statues. Above the doorways and windows and along the panels of the ceiling was a rail holding thousands of portraits staring down at us. The tour guide wasn't wrong: you could come here every day and see something you'd never noticed before. It was all on a much grander scale than the Accademia.

I was standing still, trying to take it all in, when someone touched my arm. It was an elderly woman who was part of our tour. "Come along, dear," she said in a broad Scottish accent. "Elora is waiting for us."

Elora? Had I misunderstood the tour leader when she said, "*Allora,* let's begin." Was it instead her *name*? It was a name I hadn't heard in nearly forty years but it was a name I had once known well.

The first day of grade three, a little girl had stepped into our class, our class that had been together since kindergarten. The rest of us wore our back-to-school outfits, sweltering in clothes that were far too heavy and autumnal for early September and in shiny new shoes that caused blisters on our toes and ankles, but not the new girl. She wore a silky dress that could have been a woman's shirt, covered in an elephant print, and the first pair of clogs I had ever seen. She had style that did not come out of the Sears catalogue. I felt envy twist in my gut like a kind of childish lust: I wanted to *be* her.

Our third-grade teacher going through the attendance roster said, "Elora?" Robbie G said, "Elora? Isn't that a place?" The new girl who was tiny and strawberry blonde with crinkled eyes said, "It's where I was conceived." I didn't know what *conceived* meant but I saw that she had dimples. Mrs. Balsara quickly went on to Michelle M and the rest of the class list, while Robbie G made a lewd gesture with his finger and fist so that even if we didn't know what conceived meant, we knew it had something to do with what Mrs. Balsara would explain later in the year as intercourse and what Robbie would give lurid details about at recess. But even when we didn't know the definition of the word, we knew it meant that Elora Lowe was more exotic and grown up than the rest of us would probably ever be. There was something about her that made her a star rather than a new kid.

Elora moved away at the end of grade four but her name stayed as a kind of shorthand of style for me, for a few years at least. I'd thought of her a few times since—once I was in a store in Toronto that smelled of patchouli and was filled with floaty dresses, and the little blonde fairy of a girl popped into my mind. When Gil told me about a classmate buying a Ouija board at a garage sale, I thought of Elora, and the séance she had held at her house during a sleepover. I had been glad I hadn't been invited when I heard that three girls went home in hysterics at midnight, but I was also fascinated and not altogether surprised that Elora could talk to the dead. Her eyes apparently rolled back in her head when she was contacting Elvis, and that was when the other girls began shrieking.

I heard the word as *allora* at the start of the tour of the Uffizi, never imagining it was our leader's name.

All of a sudden, I wondered if the tour leader could possibly be the same person.

I felt distracted throughout the tour, as we passed through elaborate rooms filled with equally elaborate paintings. I was focused on the tour guide, trying to see in her dark and heavy features whether she could have been the tiny blonde child I had known. I could not decide.

At the end of our tour, Elora announced she had a surprise for us and walked blithely out of the Uffizi, feather blowing in the air, past the statues in the piazza and stopped in front of a café, where every arched window declared its name.

"I always end my tours at the Caffè Rivoire, because they have the best hot chocolate in *Firenze,* and I want you to remember and tell all your friends how sweet your tour has been, on *La Dolce Vita*."

It was a cheesy and clearly rehearsed line, but it was also well-received by the group who clapped their hands as Elora gestured with her peacock feather. A waiter came out to the patio with a tray covered in tiny cups filled with rich hot chocolate. We stood, as if at a cocktail party, sipping our drinks and chatting in the mid-afternoon shadows while Elora pulled a phone out of her pocket and began checking her messages, her expression relaxing.

"Excuse me," I said. I had to say something. She looked up, her tour-guide face instantly back on again. "I have to ask you. By any chance, did you grow up in Canada? In Waterloo?"

Surprise rippled across her face and she looked at me for the first time. "I lived there for a few years. Do we know each other?"

"I think maybe," I said. "I went to Sandowne Public School."

"Oh my god," she said. "What a small world. What's your name again?"

"Liz. I'm Elizabeth Fane but I was Lizzie Baston then. We were in Mrs. Balsara's class together in grade three. You're Elora Lowe?"

"That's just crazy. Yes, that's me." She looked around and the tour had begun to disperse. "Hold on a bit. Unless you have to rush away?"

I nodded—I had all sorts of time. She spoke to one or two people, thanking them for joining the tour, explaining about another tour she did, a wine-tasting. As I waited, I took a second cup of hot chocolate—now tepid—from the tray and looked around the square at the fountain. It looked strangely familiar, and I recognized it was the fountain from *A Room with a View* in the scene where the Italian gets stabbed. I wandered over to the fountain, out of the shadows and into the light, turning to look at Elora, who motioned again that I should wait. I looked at the fountain—masculine and unchristian with its wild horses and satyrs—and I found myself looking for bloodstains from the movie, and then I dipped my hand in the water and it was colder than I expected despite the sunshine.

"There you are! I thought I'd lost you!" Elora came striding across the piazza toward me. "Can I buy you a drink?"

"Sure," I said, although I wondered what we might talk about. It was not exactly as though we were long-lost friends. But it felt good to have someone to go out with, someone from home.

As we strode along the narrow streets paved with cobblestones, Elora gave me a private tour. "Right here was where Savonarola burned all the art and books as part of the Bonfire of the Vanities . . . and down this lane—" She still held the peacock feather in her hand and was gesturing with it—"This was Dante's home. I never take tours here, but you should go sometime."

"I've been wondering what these signs are about," I said, pointing to one of the silver 1966 plaques.

"That's from *L'Alluvione,* the Flood," Elora said. "In the fall of 1966, it rained seventeen inches of rain. It was also weirdly warm that fall so the early snows in the mountains all melted. And then, some engineers decided to let out water on purpose to prevent the dam above Florence from breaking, and all that water hit Florence like a tidal wave. Twenty feet of water and mud and oil."

"Twenty feet?"

"In some places. It was different in different parts of the city. These signs are at the high-water mark to show how deep it was."

I looked at the marker above us. It was impossible to imagine the jade-green Arno flooding the streets. "That's crazy," I said.

"It was a disaster," Elora said and began walking again. I followed her as I had all day, listening. "People died. Tons of art was destroyed and there are crazy stories about art being rescued too—a museum director who swam with an original manuscript in his teeth to save it, international students they called mud angels."

She pointed. "That's my favorite gelato place. Totally touristy and crazy expensive but worth it. And here is my bar." She held open a door and I stepped inside, still trying to imagine the water from the placid river covering the city, thinking that Florence had had a Flood just like I had. Ahead of us were ancient stone stairs, rutted in the center by centuries of feet, descending into the basement where country-western music was playing.

When we got to the bottom, Elora waved at the bartender and sat down in one seat of a booth, stretching her legs out on the bench, and placing her feather on the table. I sat across from her.

"You'll never guess where I got this feather," she said. She told me the story—and it involved a poker game, a live peacock, Poland in the early '90s, and a band she had been part of—while the bartender brought her a tall beer in a glass and took my order for red wine.

When he returned with my wine, Elora interrupted the story to clink glasses with me. "*Salute*," she said. She took off her glasses, and wiped beneath her eyes with her fingertips, put her glasses back on and rested her hands on her belly as though she were pregnant.

"So," she said. "Do you still live in Sandowne? I mean, Waterloo?"

I hesitated slightly. In part it was because I felt she would look on me in judgment for never having ventured out of my hometown, and in part because my Waterloo life felt so entirely removed from Florence.

"I do actually," I said, sipping wine, which was good although not as good as the wine at the convent.

"And what does life look like in Waterloo?"

I told her briefly about Russ and the boys. I decided I wouldn't tell her about my work, partly because I didn't work there anymore. "How about you?" I asked. "How long have you been in Florence?"

She drained her beer. "Almost five years," she said. "Longest I've ever lived anywhere."

I was listening to a resumé of all the places she had lived when Elora's face lit up and she smiled, showing me the dimples I remembered. She waved and I turned to see who she was waving at. A woman with unnaturally red hair, probably ten years older than us, was descending into the bar. She came over to the table and leaned over to kiss Elora on one cheek and then the other and finally the first cheek again. They spoke briefly in Italian, and then Elora looked over at me.

"It's better if we speak English?" she said. I nodded. "This is my flatmate, Patrizia. Patrizia, this is Liz. She was on my tour this afternoon, and you will never believe it—it's such a small world—we went to school together in Canada when we were children. We were just telling each other about our lives. Come, join us. How was your day?"

Patrizia was, it turned out, a hairdresser, and there had been a client whose hair would simply not take curl that afternoon, which was why she was late. The bartender brought her a drink, in a tall thin green glass. She drank it and looked at Elora. "*Come stai?*" she said to Elora, gently. That was one of my phrases from my Italian classes. It felt exciting to recognize the language. "*Abbastanza bene*," Elora said, wrinkling up her nose as though to belie her words. I knew that answer too: it was the equivalent of a hand waggle—a tentative "okay."

I looked at my watch: it was still hours until supper at the convent but I wasn't willing to take the bus there after dark, and by now the shadows would fully be covering the piazza, and the air would be colder and purple over the hills.

"I need to get going," I said. "*Piacere*." Nice to meet you. "So nice to see you again after all these years."

"Wait," Elora said, glancing over at Patrizia. "We're taking a trip in a couple of weeks to the castles in the mountains. Will you still be here? Would you like to join us?"

"That sounds interesting," I said, "but I work most days. I have Saturday afternoons off. And Sundays."

"Patrizia only has Sundays off, and I don't do tours every single week. It would be a Sunday."

"That would work," I said. It felt satisfying to have someone want my company. "What's your number?"

Elora pointed to her phone. "I have yours," she said. "Because you came on the tour. So I'll text you and we can pick you up and show you around. There's not much to see, of course, in Italy, but we'll do our best."

She laughed and I laughed with her. An authentic *avventura*, I said to myself. As I rode the bus back to the convent, I saw that Russ had texted me, checking in to see how I was. I wrote back, telling him about the coincidence of running into an old schoolmate on a tour, how she was going to show me around.

It's a small world, he wrote, just as Elora had said earlier.

16

When our kids came to us to tell us something their brother had done, we always told them there were two kinds of telling on someone: the tattling kind where you got someone in trouble and the kind where you got someone or yourself out of trouble. Only the second kind was good.

The same was true with *not* telling, with keeping secrets.

My friend Joanna told me after her husband left her that a healthy relationship was one where there were no secrets. I nodded but I knew that wasn't the whole story. Sometimes a surprise reveal was all the more exciting than anticipation. Like the surprise trip to Disney we planned for our kids—I nearly burst with holding that secret in, and our kids were so thrilled the day we climbed into the car and told them we were on our way to the airport. Other times, a shared secret could bring people together: we opted to wait the usual three months before telling anyone of our pregnancies, keeping the joy and nervousness to ourselves.

But Joanna was right about certain kinds of secrets—the destructive ones. The building where I worked had been built over time with various additions, making it a kind of labyrinth, with some staircases not going to some floors. It seemed appropriate to me as a place of secrets. In my work as executive director "Don't tell anyone, but . . ." was a phrase I heard countless times. Many secrets could be kept in that place. Some could not. Duty to report, embezzled funds with a paper trail, a burned-out building. Some secrets would take form, reveal themselves.

Perhaps the most disturbing were those who even kept secrets from themselves. I had fired a staff member who ran our social media, who posted awful things about our work on her personal account. That person had denied it to the end with a poker face that was shocking as though she truly believed in what she was saying despite the clear evidence to the contrary. I worried about her, but we were never able to get beyond what she had decided about reality.

I had become accustomed to holding secrets in my work, at least where I could do so, but I had begun to wonder about the secrets I hid even from myself. A person didn't have to be delusional to have blind spots. I tried to be honest with myself and others, but surely I had places I didn't want to look, things I didn't want to admit even to myself. Those were dangers too.

Sometimes things hinge on a secret. In *A Room with a View*, the main character, Lucy, who faints after seeing the stabbing in the piazza, asks the young man who rescues her to keep it secret to prevent gossip. But while he does not tell anyone, he also says it is a moment when something tremendous has happened to them, that they have had a true adventure together. Sometimes a secret shared is simple and occasionally it is serious. Either way, trust is delicate. Later in the film when the man kisses her, they are seen by Lucy's chaperone who swears her to secrecy but the chaperone herself does not keep the secret and it comes out in a way that alters Lucy's life forever.

Some secrets are good and some are bad. But they are always powerful, and they can always change everything.

17

NICCOLÒ SLUNG HIS ARM OVER A BRANCH OF AN OLIVE tree as though putting an arm around an old friend. I had seen him touch trees in passing, speak soothingly to damaged or young trees, and stand on the terrace surveying the whole of the grove with pride. Salvia explained to Honey and me that to Niccolò the trees were like his children. Every morning, like the first morning, he would drink a small shot glass of green olive oil before we began work, offering thanks first with an upraised arm—I presumed to God—and then with a sweep of his hand and a nod of his head to the grove.

"His *magnum opus*," I said one day to Honey as we saw him above us on the terrace, surveying the grove of trees.

"His what?" she said.

"*Charlotte's Web*," I said. "Did you never read the book?"

She had seen the movie. I remembered reading the book aloud to the boys. In so many books the heroes were orphans or had escaped their parents but in this one, the mother was a hero. When I read that book to the boys, I had to explain why I got choked up when Charlotte, dying, made certain her egg sac—her *magnum opus*—survived her, just as she had made sure that Wilbur the pig would live.

I got a catch in my throat even as I told Honey about it while we dragged sticks to the fire pit. I thought of my own *magnum opus*: my three sons. I had heard back from them in a variety of brief texts that felt both utterly familiar and completely unsatisfying, texts that were too casual to match the intensity of my heart.

What Honey focused on was not the story itself but the fact that I had read such a long book to my children. "For my mom," she said, rolling her eyes, "there was too much repetition in *Goodnight Moon*. She always cut to the chase. I can't believe you read the whole thing out loud."

"We didn't read it all in one night."

"Still."

I readjusted my hair in my baseball cap. The irony had not been lost on me that after only two weeks of pruning olive trees, I found myself desperate for a haircut. I had worn my hair the same way for years—all one length about halfway between my chin and my shoulders as I would tell my hairdresser—and I got it trimmed just a week before I came to Italy, but here the cut didn't work. Maybe the Italian water acted differently on my hair. I wasn't sure but I did know that my natural wave had disappeared and my hair hung lank and heavy. It wasn't long enough to wear in a ponytail and yet it stuck to the back of my neck so that by the time we stopped for lunch each day, I felt straggly and grubby. I'd found a baseball cap a former volunteer had left behind and I had taken to stuffing as much of my hair into it as possible. I wondered whether I could get a haircut from Elora's roommate.

That evening I downloaded *Charlotte's Web* on my phone. When Honey was setting herself on the orange couch and flipping to one of the game shows we had taken to watching, I asked her if she wanted a surprise. She muted the tv and I began to read.

Honey rubbed my feet with olive oil as she listened. I had been terribly shy the first time she offered to do this, even though I'd had a pedicure before I left home. Feet seemed ugly and personal. But Honey was gentle and hadn't laughed. The woman who had been at the convent before me apparently knew reflexology and had taught Cecy and Honey all about it.

"Although," Honey laughed, "if you asked Cecy, every part of the foot corresponded with something sexual."

Something unwound in me as Honey kneaded my feet like dough and we had quickly slipped into a routine that reminded me of my grandmother and her sister, who shared a house, watching *Wheel of Fortune* while eating dinner on tv trays.

We would climb the marble steps after each feast of a supper, my knees protesting, my stomach filled with extraordinary food and wine. We would stop on the covered walkway, which I discovered was called a *loggia,* to say goodnight to the world, and especially to our olive trees. We would count how many we'd pruned, breathing in the smells of the night, the cool, damp night shot through by stars and star-like points of light on the hills around the city. I would silently blow a kiss in the western direction, to Russ and the boys. Then we'd collapse on the couch and put on the television and watch it the way you might watch a traffic accident: filled with horror but also curiosity, unable to look away, trying to dissect what might be happening. The language was rapid-fire quick and slangy, making us realize how truly unskilled we were in our Italian.

That night I read three chapters aloud. Italian gameshows flashed across the screen in ever-changing, never-changing garish scenes while Fern nursed the runt of the litter, bathed her baby pig in buttermilk, and Charlotte greeted him with salutations.

When I finished the chapter, Honey sighed, "If my parents had read me books like this, I might not have joined the carnival."

After the last six months I had little judgment left in me. "They probably tried their best like all of us," I said, putting the book down and pulling her foot into my lap.

18

No one told me in advance that on the third day after childbirth, as a mother's milk came in, so too did a flood of hormones and emotions. I found myself engorged and sobbing three days after Timothy was born. The object of my tears was something no one had to tell me about: "Someday," I wailed, "someday, he's going to grow up and leave us."

Now it had happened. They had all gone. And it had been bad but it had not been the worst part.

After the worst happened, a friend hosted a painting party in the fall, and she invited me. I imagined myself going, imagined myself covering the canvas in thick black paint, covering myself in black paint. I imagined squeezing an entire tube of red paint into the middle of the canvas, like a tube of toothpaste, like blood, like afterbirth. I decided I could not bring myself to go to the painting party, and when I saw the painted bouquets of cheerful daisies and wildflowers afterwards, and contrasted them with my own visions, I was glad I had not. But I was almost tempted to buy the paints to make my vision a reality.

I tried to explain myself to Russ more than once. The problem was that Russ was infinitely practical: if something could be done, he would do it gladly, but if nothing could apparently be done, then why would someone spend time thinking about it?

I couldn't *not* think about it. I'd heard about a phenomenon called "last-egg syndrome" where menopausal women craved having a baby and perhaps that was why I couldn't stop thinking about it, why I held the cats more than I should have, their soft small bodies, their purring a comfort. Sometimes, I wandered around the house, simply carrying a cat, as though it were a baby. I found myself doing the new parent jostle with the cats, the sway that would stop a baby from crying, the movement that a parent found so instinctively.

19

As I crossed the Ponte Vecchio the next Saturday, I saw no fewer than five flower sellers, each stocking one type of flower only—bouquets of brilliant yellow pompom flowers. I hadn't noticed the flower sellers before, but perhaps I'd been focused on the dazzling displays of gold in the windows. This was a city of layers, and each time I walked it, I found new details to marvel at.

I went on into the city and I saw more such bouquets, many people carrying the same flowers. Clearly this was a thing, even if I could understand it no better than I could the game shows.

"*Quanto costa?*" I asked the next flower vendor I saw, a man with very dark skin. The bouquets were not outrageously priced, so I bought myself some. "*Come si chiama?*" I asked the vendor, feeling hopeful that I was asking what the flowers were called, and not what he himself was called.

"Mimosa," he said. I wanted to ask him what they were for, what the occasion was but my six weeks of Italian had not gone that far. "*Perché?*" I asked. Why? He shrugged and explained that he himself was not Italian. I walked on with my bouquet. I smelled it but it was odorless.

I had decided that my destination for the afternoon was the Dante Museum Elora had pointed out to me as we were walking for drinks the previous week. I began by finding my way back to the Uffizi courtyard where Elora's tour had met, and then into the piazza where she served us hot chocolate at the end of the tour.

I heard my name being called twice before I turned. When I saw Elora waving as she gathered people for a tour, I realized it wasn't as unlikely as it might have seemed: I was retracing my steps and she was leading the same tour.

"Are you going to join us again?" she asked, with a dimpled smile. She too carried a small bouquet of the flowers, tucked into her belt, the only color on a black background. I also remembered what she had said about the Uffizi, that you could spend a year just looking at the floors and ceilings of the museum. But I didn't have a year: I was already two weeks into my time away.

I told her I was going to go to the Dante Museum. "Great choice," she said. Then she paused. "Want to come over for brunch tomorrow?"

It would mean another Sunday of not going to the English Church for services. "Where and what time?"

"I'll text you," she said and turned to her group.

I had told myself I could join the nuns any morning for their early morning mass, but I hadn't done that any more than I had gone to the English Church. I was fully adjusted to the time zone, and my fatigue from pruning trees meant that I was sound asleep by ten every night and wide awake by the time they sang their mass in the morning, but every day I found another reason not to join them.

Most afternoons I walked up the hill to San Miniato to listen to the monks sing their mass, but the nuns felt different. At San Miniato there were benches with kneelers for those who knew how to participate in the mass—those, say, who knew whether the monks were singing in Latin or Italian. I had no idea. I sat on the cold marble stairs and let the unknown words wash over me, thinking of the Bible verse about how when we struggle to pray, God expresses our pain in groans beyond words. The monks were not wordless but aside from the occasional *Jesu Christi*, to me, they might as well have been and yet their singing somehow expressed the pain I could not articulate.

I could watch the monks in their white robes at a remove, as though the fence they sang behind created distance, like a stage with a curtain that separated the actors from the audience. There was no area for spectators in the nuns' chapel. I felt as though they would look on me with disapproval if I joined them and didn't know when to sit or stand or cross myself. Even as I passed them in the hallways, some of the nuns looked at me as though I wasn't welcome. Some of them were probably about my age, and I wondered how they had chosen to be there. Salvia was the youngest and by far the most welcoming—she was the only one who introduced herself—although there was one very elderly nun who was nearly bent double with age, and yet who wore the happiest smile. That nun always carried our bread to us at meals, following either the "*mangia mangia*" nun or the dour beetle-browed nun who brought us our main courses. The *mangia mangia* nun was always careful to hold the swinging door for the elderly nun, but the beetle-browed nun would hurry back through the door, so the elderly nun had to stop to be sure it wasn't going to hit her in the face. I was afraid of what that nun would do if I didn't stand at the right time in the mass.

Now in the Uffizi courtyard, I decided that if Elora didn't text me about brunch, I would go to the English Church. Before that, I would find Dante.

As I headed in the direction we'd gone the previous week, I saw more of the flood signs but I couldn't find the little turn that led to the street where the house was. I should have asked Elora for the address. I stopped and found a bench in a small piazza and reached into my purse for my phone. It wasn't there. I looked again and again, but it still wasn't there. Had I been pickpocketed? My wallet was still there. Had I dropped it? Had

I left it in my room? I thought of what the writer C. S. Lewis had said about grief being like quitting smoking, that he thought he could do it if only he had what he craved. I thought I would be fine without my phone, if only I had my phone to call the convent to check if it was there, or to use it to find directions for where I was supposed to be going. I hadn't brought the astronomer's map either.

I decided to keep going. This was a small town after all. Either I would find the museum or I would find my way back to the convent. I told myself that. But the buildings all began to look the same, and so did the streets. It felt like a maze. My heart began to beat faster.

I reached an area where there was a string of cafes and bars. I stuck my head into the first one, and was greeted with a roar of cheers, as though they had all been waiting for me. It was disconcerting. I went up to the bar. "Dante's House?" I said. "*Casa di Dante?*" The bartender shrugged and threw up his hands in apology for not knowing, although I wasn't sure whether he didn't know English, couldn't understand my attempts at Italian or didn't know where the house was.

When I came out into the street again, I couldn't decide which direction to go. A group of women, more than slightly tipsy, arms around one another, dark hair strung with garlands made of the same yellow flowers, came toward me on the sidewalk.

"*Buona festa, signora!*" they called to me loudly, insistently. "*Buona festa!*" They kept yelling at me and seemed to expect something in return.

I had no idea what they wanted from me. It was one thing for the monks to sing prayers I didn't understand but here on the streets the strangeness of the language felt aggressive and slightly out of control.

Somehow despite my Italian classes and despite the fact that this was actually Italy, I had not fully grasped how immersed I would be in Italian until I lived in it. I spoke English with Honey, of course, and with Salvia and Niccolò, but the other nuns spoke no English at all, and unless I signed up for an explicitly English tour—as I had with Elora—I had to assume I was swimming in the sea that was the Italian language. And though it was a beautiful sea, sometimes—like now—I longed desperately for the shore of home.

For the first time, I felt the aloneness of where I was. I touched my sternum and was relieved I had my whistle on, but I wondered how people would respond if I ever used it. Would they understand that it was a signal for help or would they break into laughter?

I needed to find the museum. I found a small *tabacchi* and the person inside mercifully spoke some English and had a map of central Florence. My breath still quickened, I ran a finger over the map until I saw where I had taken a jog in the street to be a turn.

"*Grazie*," I said, imprinting the map on my memory and taking off at a faster pace. I felt relief as I saw the road signs I needed, and then the little road I should have taken. Within five minutes I was entering the Dante Museum and on shaky legs stumbling up the stairs to the entrance. There, behind glass, looking for all the world like someone selling tickets to a movie or a circus, sat a terribly bored young woman.

I paid and stepped inside. It was a warm day for March—it felt more like May or even June at home—but the day in no way explained the dampness of my hair on my neck. I lifted it and then it fell heavily back into place as I paced around the first room of the museum.

I was too shaky to take it in. There were samples of different plants grown in Florence, a map of medieval Florence, complete with walls and sections of the city. There were explanations about how in medieval times Florence's families had lived in multi-floored towers that somehow saved them from fire, and which could be added to or dismantled at will. There was a dagger that *could have* belonged to Dante. Every display had an explanatory sign, but the explanations were paragraphs long and my eyes were still swimming from having lost my way.

I went up another set of stairs—realizing that this was, in fact, one of the medieval towers—and I heard strange dissonant music coming from ahead of me. It was a video playing to an empty room, a retelling of the *Divine Comedy.*

There were no chairs in the room so I sat down on the floor, leaning against a wall, my hair still sweaty and plastered to the back of my neck as weird images and sounds representing hell flashed across the screen. As my heart slowed to a more normal pace, I saw cats in this cinematic vision and I wondered if they—and I—were both alive and dead.

It wasn't until later that night, sitting in my room at the convent, my yellow flowers stuck into a water glass underneath the portrait of Mary and beside my phone—which, it turned out, I had left plugged in that morning—that I thought of the irony that I had gotten lost on my way to find Dante.

"You wouldn't have gotten lost, would you?" I said to Mary, irritated at her looking down at me, her being literally and figuratively above me. "You're annoyingly perfect," I said, and she only smiled in response.

I wouldn't get lost again either if I could help it. The next morning, having received a text with an address and time from Elora, I triple-checked I had my phone with me, and called for a taxi to take me to Elora's apartment, which was not far from the central train station.

Right before I left I realized I should bring a hostess gift, but I had no idea what to bring. I had bought a couple of souvenirs at San Miniato, but I wasn't at all sure I should bring a CD of Gregorian chant or a small wooden cross to Elora Lowe.

Then I remembered that, inside their office, the nuns had a display of lacework they made, and small bottles of their olive oil, both of which they sold to the guests. It was what we used for our foot massages.

"You could probably take some and pay them later," Honey said.

I might be skipping church yet again, but I wasn't about to steal from the nuns. There was one very small unopened bottle in our little kitchenette, although I had no idea how old it was. I grabbed it and then ran down the stairs and out to the front of the house where my taxi was waiting.

Elora and Patrizia lived above the hair salon where Patrizia worked, not far from the train station. I could smell bacon as I entered the apartment.

"Did you make this yourself?" Elora asked when I handed it to her. Patrizia came and kissed me on both cheeks as I said that no, I was just pruning the trees, but that it was from my nuns' olive grove.

Elora explained that sometimes she liked to make a North American brunch, rather than the typical Italian breakfast. In addition to the typical bread and jam and coffee, she had cooked scrambled eggs, as well as bacon and a beautiful cake covered in chunks of another golden cake and held together with lemon cream.

In the center of the table in the dining room was an enormous bouquet of the same yellow flowers.

"What are these flowers about?" I asked. "They're everywhere."

"International Women's Day," Elora said. "They really celebrate it here. Although it was yesterday."

"It's a day for women to celebrate women," Patrizia said. She spoke with a strong Italian accent but her English was perfect. "People give mimosa flowers to women. Sometimes we celebrate it by going to strip clubs or getting drunk. *Festa della donna. Buona festa.*"

I thought of the women outside the bar who had yelled those words at me the day before, words I now reinterpreted as wishing me well, even if the well-wishers were drunk.

As we ate, they told me about Florence, about the difference between tourist and local life, but how so few locals were able to afford to live in the core of the city anymore. They talked about the influx of tourists who came to Florence the week before Easter and stayed until the rains began in September.

"We shouldn't complain," Elora said. "Tourists put this food on the table. I say God bless 'em."

I asked them to explain about the game shows Honey and I watched, although their explanations seemed as bizarre as the shows themselves. As they talked, I kept thinking about how badly I needed a haircut, but I wasn't sure whether it would be too awkward to ask. After they wouldn't let me wash dishes at the end of the meal, I decided to venture my question.

"My hair is driving me crazy. It's the wrong length for working outside," I said. "Could I maybe make an appointment with you next weekend to get it cut?"

"I will be happy to cut your hair," Patrizia said, standing up. "*Allora*. Let's go."

"No, no," I said. "Not on your day off. I meant maybe one afternoon after I'm done work." The monks at San Miniato could do without me for a day.

Patrizia insisted and began to make me feel like it was a question of hospitality.

"Have fun, kids," Elora said, stretching her legs out, her hands clasped on top of her stomach. "I'm going to sit here and drink and smoke while you work."

Patrizia led me down the fire escape and to the back door of the salon. The room was darkened as the blinds were closed over the windows. She didn't open them but pointed me toward a chair in front of a sink. She wrapped a plastic smock around my shoulders and tilted my chin back, adjusting the water to warm. The shampoo she used was strongly scented with what might have been gardenias or lilacs.

She led me to a seat in the front of the salon, turned on the single light over her chair and flicked on a radio. I was prepared to explain what I wanted and started to describe it, but Patrizia didn't make eye contact with me. She instead began combing my hair, staring intently at my face and running her hands over my skull. A rhythmic song beat out from the radio. I looked at my own face, with the single light shining down on me; it was full of hollows, my eyes hidden in shadows.

Patrizia clipped my hair up at the back of my head and began cutting. My head was bowed and I could see from the length of the pieces of brown hair that fell on the ground around me that she was giving me far more than a trim. I thought of my first salon haircut as a child—how my head had ended up looking like a shingled roof. Then I thought of how my hair had been plastered to my neck while I worked and decided it would be worth it no matter how it looked. There were weeks until I went home—it would have time to grow out. I wondered what my hairdresser at home, would say. I tried to recognize the photos Patrizia had stuck up around her mirror: there was one of her with Mickey Mouse and another with George Clooney. None of the others were recognizable—they could have been friends, clients, or even Italian movie stars.

Another song came to an end as Patrizia began using a razor blade to thin my hair. She stopped to survey her work, then picked up a pair of electric clippers and proceeded to shave the back of my neck.

She opened a jar and rubbed something on her hands, then ran her fingers through my hair. Product, my kids would call it. She turned on a hair dryer, more to blow the bits of hair away from me as my hair was already almost dry.

"*Bella?*" she said, hands on hips.

It was disconcerting—just as I had found an enormous difference in being Elizabetta as the *suore* called me, so it was a very different version of myself looking back at me from the mirror. Fortunately, I looked neither like a shingled roof nor like the shorn olive trees. I liked it. My hair swung forward around my face but graduated to an almost-but-not-quite brush cut at the back. It was the most stylish cut I'd ever had but also looked like it suited me. I had seen women before, women I wanted to stop to say: your hair completely suits you. Now I was one of them.

"How much?" I asked Patrizia as she swept the floor and she waved me off, but it was my turn to insist. I had a fifty euro note in my purse—for emergencies—and while this was not a crisis, it certainly felt like some sort of emergence as though unexpectedly I was becoming a new person. That hadn't been my intention in coming to Italy—I had wanted a safe cocoon to process what had happened and to heal. I hadn't counted on growing new wings.

I found my purse when I went upstairs and handed the bill to Patrizia. "*Grazie,*" I said.

Elora, who was relaxing with a drink and a cigarette, approved of my haircut from the comfort of her couch. "Two weeks from today," she said. "We're going to the castles near Canossa. Want to join us?"

As I nodded, my hair bounced differently. I remembered how I had identified with mourning practices last fall, how I had understood why people in other cultures put ashes on their heads, tore their clothes, shaved their heads. Somehow you needed to enact grief in your body. I hadn't done that then—although it was what I had done in my garden. But I was still grieving now, and this short haircut seemed both culturally appropriate and somehow symbolically important as an expression that I was no longer who I had been. Niccolò had said you wouldn't get olive oil without extreme pruning—I hoped this haircut might lead me back to life as well as simply allowing me to work without my hair distracting me.

The next day I wore the baseball cap but I didn't need to stuff my hair into it. By the end of the day I had a sunburn on the back of my neck, an area that hadn't seen the sun for more than thirty-five years. I rubbed a drop of olive oil into it after I showered. I worried I wouldn't be able to reproduce the way Patrizia had styled my hair, concerned that without product in my hair, I would look like a shingled roof, but it was a miracle: my hair fell into the same stylish shape.

I got a haircut! I texted my friend Karin.

Do you like it? she wrote back.

I do. I look like Elizabetta.

Elizabetta?

That's what the nuns call me.

20

Every year since the boys were small, every Christmas we gave them a Matchbox car among their stocking stuffers. As I tucked the little cars into their stockings last December, it hit me, a tsunami of emotion. It seemed like it had all passed in the blink of an eye, that I almost might be putting the first cars in their stockings. It was what older women always said, "Enjoy every minute. It goes so fast." The Good Mother response to those women was to grimace politely and escape before you blew up at them. I wasn't sure when I crossed the line from younger to older. I hadn't resisted getting older. I had been almost entirely unaware of the fact. I could tell you—at first in weeks, then months, and now years—exactly how old my kids were, but I had to pause and subtract my birth year from the calendar year to remember my own age. I had heard women lament becoming invisible as they got older, but I had no idea whether I was or wasn't.

Until last fall when suddenly they were all gone.

I remembered very clearly being their age, stretching my wings in a new city, with the sense that the entire world was opening up to me. It was one of the best feelings of my life and I would not for a moment take that away from my kids. The challenge for me was that I was no longer part of something new and exciting.

"Mothering is the only job," I lamented to my friend Joanna, "where if you're good at it, you get fired."

"More like retired."

"Yeah . . . thanks," I said, not feeling grateful.

When I had found myself at loose ends this past September, after Gil moved away to college, I knitted enormous sweaters for each of the boys in their university colors. But by the time December came and I wrapped them, they felt almost entirely foreign to me, as though someone else had made them. The holidays were strange. I was numb and tiptoeing, trying not to stub my toe on any landmines.

As I watched them open their presents, I saw their delight and also how unable they were to see me or to see that I might have a life beyond them. Honestly, I wasn't sure I did either, and I hated the sweaters. They seemed needy and clingy, desperate rather than loving. And why hadn't I knit one for Russ or for myself?

21

SOMETIME IN THE MIDDLE OF THE NIGHT I JOLTED AWAKE in bed as the sound of something immense cracked open. By the time I even opened my eyes, my convent room was illuminated by the next bolt of lightning and more crashing sounds immediately on top of the flash of light, tearing open the night. The light illuminated the face of Mary on the wall opposite me again and again, although she looked calm and even amused. I heard the wind pick up into a terrible howl and rain or possibly sleet began smashing itself against my window. I got up to close the window and looked out to see another flash show the cypresses swaying in the gale.

The tiniest knock came at my door. I assumed it was Honey, awakened by the storm but when I opened the door, it was Salvia. She was small and girlish, bird-like with sweet brown eyes and a gentle smile.

"I will be checking your windows, that they are open just a little," she said. As she reopened the window I had just closed, I realized it was the first time I had seen her dark hair exposed, although she wore her blue habit as usual. "A little open prevents the windows from—" She moved her hands as if to show an explosion, just as another crash of lightning came. She started at the sound, put her hand over her heart and then laughed at herself. "We are safe. Also," she slipped a hand into her pocket. "I bring you a *tè*. Good for the nerves."

She handed a packet to me and it was chamomile tea. I had never drunk chamomile tea before, but it was the bedtime tea in many of the children's books I had read to the boys.

As Salvia slipped into Honey's room and the empty bedrooms to be sure the windows were open, I went out to our little kitchen and filled up the kettle. The flashes of lightning came as frequently as I waited for the kettle to boil, but there was a longer lag between the light and the thunder. The storm was moving through. I could hear it echoing around the valley like the long, low growl of an animal. I thought of one of the stories we always told about Tim, about the time he had looked up in disgust during a thunderstorm and said, "What is God *doing* up there?"

Salvia came out of the last bedroom and put a finger to her lips. "She is sleeping."

I shook my head, amazed. "Tea?"

She paused and then agreed. I poured the hot water over the tea and the faintest smell of apples and something like new-mown hay came to my nose. I handed her a cup and pointed at the orange couch, inviting to her to sit and join me, conscious that this was the first time I had hosted anyone in weeks.

There were so many questions I wanted to ask but she seemed as unapproachable and remote as the picture of Mary in my room. I wondered how she had learned to speak English, whether she ever found it lonely living among a group of nuns, most of whom were old enough to be her mother. I wondered how she had chosen to be a nun, whether she had ever wanted to marry and have children, whether she ever had second thoughts about her choices.

"*Grazie*," she said, cupping her hands around the tea. I sat beside the window with my cup, watching as the lightning lit up the olive grove, an undulating sea of gray-green leaves in the storm.

I sipped my tea and it was every bit as nice as Peter Rabbit had said. When I looked back at Salvia, she held in her hand what I realized was a rosary and was mouthing prayers. My temptation was to mother her, to wrap a blanket around her shoulders, to tell her it would be all right, but I saw the tension leave her face as she prayed. She set the beads in her lap and drank more tea. As the storm rumbled on, I asked her some of my questions and she replied with quiet little answers.

When the storm was over, she drained her cup and carried it to the sink where she rinsed it. "*Grazie*," she said again, and slipped out of our apartment and back to the convent.

I heard another rumble of thunder in the distance, in the next valley, at least. What *was* God doing up there? I wondered again about the little nun. I tried to imagine myself as a nun and I couldn't. Being a mother was so deeply woven into the fabric of who I was that it didn't feel like a stretch to see it as my vocation.

The question was what became of a mother when her children grew up. A nun signed on for life but being a mother, in many ways, was only for a season. And then what?

I fell asleep with that question in my mind, the chamomile apparently as effective as advertised, and I dreamed about the nun who said *mangia, mangia* feeding me.

When I woke up, the weather was clear and so was my mind. I lay in bed and counted, like rosary beads of a sort. It was more than three weeks since I arrived in Italy and thirty-three days since my last period. I looked over at the Virgin Mary on the wall. The only other time I ever missed a period was when I was pregnant. Now I looked up at Mary with one eyebrow raised: "How can this be?" I said aloud to her, echoing her question, although with irony. I knew full well I was not pregnant, unless the power of the Most High had overshadowed me while I slept at the convent. And that was something I thought I would probably remember.

For a good week now I had felt as though my period was about to start. It felt as if a storm was brewing and humidity was building past the point when you thought the storm must break, when you dropped with humidity and headache.

It was unsettling. I had assumed for days that it had been delayed because I was working outside, because I was living on the far side of the world, because I was doing hard manual labor, because I was living with another woman. Any of these things could have thrown my body off like a kind of jet lag.

This morning, though, was like the morning when I woke up and simply knew I was pregnant with Timothy, as though his existence had been announced, days before I could take a pregnancy test. This time I knew that for the first time, I had missed a period altogether, like the shadow side of The Flood. The start of fertility's waning.

When Honey and I went down for breakfast together, the dining room was filled with a group of British tourists who had arrived the day before. They were buzzing with excitement about the olive grove having been hit badly by lightning.

When we went outside after breakfast, we found that the reports were slightly exaggerated, but a large limb had been blown off one of the biggest trees, due to a lightning strike, and when it fell, it took out two other trees and damaged another one badly.

Niccolò brought three other monks and a chainsaw with him. We spent the morning pruning, being extra careful of our footing on the wet bark, while the sounds of the chainsaw reverberated around us as the felled trees were cut apart to be sold for wood.

The big tree struck by lightning was different—the lightning had traveled right through it. I touched the tree where the limb had blown off and it was still warm, its heart blackened and smoky. I thought of the ashes and the crosses on Ash Wednesday and I made the sign of the cross on my hand. I looked at the limb on the ground and saw that the lightning had traveled along certain branches, that they too were blackened inside.

I remembered the first time I got my period, the sense of deep disappointment that *this* would happen to my body again and again and again for what felt like forever. It was a Saturday in late October and I had been given the job of raking the leaves, which just as suddenly as a result of their own internal clocks, had decided it was time to fall. The lawn was carpeted in gold. I felt vaguely nauseous as I pushed them into a pile my father would later burn. I had read *Are You There God, It's Me Margaret* as all the girls my age had but that didn't fully prepare me and it seemed like any other Saturday until it wasn't.

When I went to church the next day, I heard the word blood in the worship several times and I felt like I was closer to God somehow. Now this missing period felt like the opposite. I was as conscious of my body as I was then, with the same sense of "so this thing I've heard about is really happening to me."

"How old were the trees?" I asked Niccolò, who only shrugged. "And what happens now?" He looked at me quizzically as though the answer were obvious. "We plant again. We wait until the risk of frost is no more and then we plant new trees."

I gathered several of the smaller blackened branches and put them beside my water bottle. Later I brought them to my room and put them in a jar beside the glass with mimosas in it under the painting of Mary, and my room took on the faintest scent of lightning.

22

I DECIDED NOT TO TELL MY MOTHER WHEN I GOT MY FIRST period for fear for how she would understand it.

I remembered how when I was a small child, one day my mother had sat down beside me on the couch and handed me a small book with blank colorful pages as though she had been desperately waiting to share it with me for years. Which was probably true. She grew up in the heyday of the evangelical church, after the Second World War, at a time when Billy Graham offered revival meetings and four spiritual laws, and this Wordless Book was the way people of her vintage and beliefs led small children to faith. I can recall how the white page was next to the black page as a way of telling us our sin separated us from God. The red represented the blood of Jesus, the green, new life in Christ, and lastly the gold told us about heaven.

For my mother, it really was—and is—that simple. Her hope is so secure that it is almost certainty. In one sense it is entirely lovely.

The problem is that it never made space for complexities and it didn't make a lot of room for humanity. I was a "thorn in the flesh" to her until I realized—even as a child—that my questions and complexities truly upset her. Anything complex belonged strictly on the black page of the wordless book. Surely I'd had bad dreams as a child, and surely she came to me and rocked and soothed me—for how else would I have known how to do it with my boys—but I don't remember either any bad dreams or any soothing arms.

I worried she would see my period like the black page in the book.

I never rejected that faith but even at a young age I felt a kind of protectiveness toward her and respect for her small, wordless-book world. She prayed for me, prayed to a God I hoped could translate between her simple prayers and my difficult challenges. Yet it left me hollow, the feeling that I couldn't go to my mother for advice, that couldn't share my joys and sorrows with her.

When my father died, my mother barely missed a beat, so certain was she of his place in heaven. The day I found her in tears, trying to start the lawnmower—a task that had always been my father's—she was quick to blame her tears on her "sin nature." She accepted the casseroles people from the church brought her—this was what people with "new life" did for one another—but while she made space in her freezer for stroganoff, she didn't make space in her heart for grief. I know this because I asked her. I know this because she barely understood the question.

In the face of any tricky situation she would say, "They need Jesus." Or, "I have Jesus." At some level, I couldn't argue with her. Probably all my thoughts and theories and best practices came down to more or less the same thing, although I felt like answering that way let people off the hook more than Jesus would probably like.

But it was one thing to manage my regular life without a shoulder to lean on, and another last fall when everything fell apart. I couldn't see it as anything other than the real black page of the wordless book—but I didn't want the red page, the blood paying the penalty of sin. I wanted a blue page, the color of tears, the color of my mom's favorite sweater. I wanted a blue page shaped into arms that would hold me tight and rock me back and forth as I had done with the boys when they were small and had had a nightmare, reassuring them that everything would be all right in the morning, that it was safe to sleep.

23

My phone buzzed in the middle of the night, and I sprang from my single bed to get it, assuming, as I always did, that something was wrong with one of the boys. But it was Elora.

Not feeling well.

Postponing trip to the castles.

Sorry.

Two weeks from now?

I lay awake for more than an hour, disappointed I would have no excuse for not visiting the English Church in the morning. I assumed Russ was still going to our church at home, but I hadn't asked him, partly because I didn't want to explain why I had missed church four Sundays in a row. My stomach tightened at the thought that I was halfway through my trip. We might be more than halfway through our pruning, but I didn't feel half-ready to go home.

As I tossed and turned, I thought about why I had come, the pain raw in the night as pain always was. It was my first bout of insomnia in Italy.

Eventually I fell back asleep as the sky was lightening. I woke up late from a strange dream about one of the nuns rocking me in an enormous rocking chair. By then breakfast was over and the English church service had already started.

"Sorry," I said to Mary on the wall as though she were my mother and I was a teenager, disappointing her by skipping church. Other than the teenaged part, perhaps it was true. But I didn't care: I still felt tender and full of emotion.

I went out to the little kitchenette to see what we might have that I could eat. Honey came out of her room, shaking newly painted fingernails. We were still pruning trees, and painting nails felt premature to me.

"Hey," she said. "I thought you were going with your friend out into the country?"

"She's sick so we postponed." I pulled out a wedge of cheese from the fridge. "Is this edible? How old is it?"

Honey examined it. "It's not mine, so if you didn't buy it, I'd say it's pretty old."

I decided to stick to my dwindling pile of granola bars. I ate one as Honey looked through the fridge for other things we should throw out.

"So what are you going to do today?" I asked her.

"I don't know," she said. "You?"

"I don't know either," I said. "But it looks like a beautiful day. And I'm more than halfway through my trip so I don't want to waste it." Or sit alone with my thoughts. I could be dead and alive simultaneously if I kept busy with pruning during the week and being a tourist on the weekends.

"I've only got a couple weeks left before I hit the maximum stay here," she said. I had forgotten there was a maximum. "Hey, I know exactly what we should do. The Pinocchio Park. Tell me you won't kick yourself if you never go there while you're here. You'll be an old lady, always wondering."

I wasn't sure that would be the case, but I shrugged agreement. "When do they leave?"

"Soon," she said. "I'll go tell them we're going to come. You get ready."

In all my imaginings about Italy and all the stories I'd been told and movies I'd seen, I never thought I would end up packed into a large extended van with nuns, driving along the highway toward the Mediterranean on our way to the strangest theme park I had ever heard of. I looked out the window as we went. Elora and Patrizia had said that the old city of Florence had become impossibly expensive for locals to live in, and now the suburban neighborhoods we passed showed me where the full-time residents actually lived.

Then we were in the countryside, low hills and mountains rising around us, all punctuated with cypress trees as if they were exclamation points.

"We don't have cypresses in Canada," I said to Salvia who sat next to me. Honey was sitting near the front of the bus, with one of the larger nuns, a woman with a broad face who took up most of the seat. Honey always referred to this nun as Sister Meemaw, after her grandmother who had had the same figure.

Salvia looked surprised. "Not even in your . . . *cimetero*? For the dead?"

"No," I said. "Maybe the snow would be too much. Why in a cemetery?"

She shook her head, trying to figure out how to explain herself. She shrugged. "They are trees for sadness. For the sadness of death."

"Grief?" I said. I felt low that day. Was it grief?

"*Sì.*"

I was quiet for a few minutes, wondering whether I would have been in a better mood if I had gone with Elora and Patrizia for the day.

"Elizabetta," Salvia said shyly. "You have children, yes? Tell me about them."

I started to tell her about my sons, and she asked how old they were, and what they did. I was starting to explain about Tim being in school to become a doctor when my phone buzzed.

Sister Meemaw is offering me mints from her pocket, Honey texted. *I now know she* is *my reincarnated grandmother. DO I TELL HER SO?*

"Do you have brothers and sisters?" I asked Salvia.

"*Sì*," she said. "I am the girl and I have four brothers."

"Is your mother happy that you are a . . . *suora*?" I asked.

She giggled. "She says she always pray that one of her sons will be a priest, and it is me. That God is surprising."

Honey texted again. *DO I EAT THE MINTS?*

"And did you always know that you wanted to be a nun?" I asked.

She looked at me with her big eyes. "I want to have many children," she said. "When I am a girl, I am afraid God will call me to be a nun."

I smiled ruefully.

"No," she said, smiling. "I have many children now. I teach English to the children in the school. I have many, many children."

My phone buzzed again. *WWPD? (WHAT WOULD PINOCCHIO DO?)*

The nun driving the bus pulled off the highway and onto a small side road. I saw a sign with an enormous Pinocchio on it, his nose pointing the direction.

"How is it that the *suore* go to the Pinocchio Park?" I asked Salvia my burning question. "It doesn't sound like something nuns would do."

"Elizabetta," she said, playfully, "nuns can have the fun too. But it is a strange story. We depend on the charity of people. Our convent is given to the *suore* by a benefactor. It is a villa before this. And we have another benefactor, a cousin of Suor Angelica, who gives us the freedom to come to the Pinocchio Park."

"Can you say no?" The words slipped out of my mouth without thinking as I saw a second Pinocchio, this time with his arm around a cricket that didn't look like the Disney version of Jiminy Cricket.

"We like to say yes when we can," she said.

And then, we were there.

It was not what I expected. I had thought it might be a kind of small theme park, a miniature Disney World, but it was more of a sculpture park, with metal statues telling the story of Pinocchio. It reminded me very much of a place we went to with the boys when they were young, a botanical garden halfway between our house and Russ's parents' house. For us, it was a place where they could run off their energy safely and have a bathroom break. We always figured it was kind of boring for the boys, a better alternative than an unbroken car ride, but nothing special. Until one time, Russ suggested we stop at a McDonald's Playland instead, and the boys protested, saying that we had to go to the gardens. We stopped at the gardens on the way home from Russ's mother's funeral four years ago, and the boys were full of memories about the cedar maze there, the pond that was always full of frogs and from which they once snuck out a pair of tadpoles in a water bottle, the statue Tim had persuaded his brothers came to life at night, the greenhouse that had carnivorous plants.

As I waited to get off the bus I thought about that garden and that time in our lives, an ache growing in my chest. Honey was waiting for me, mint in her hand. "I couldn't say no to Sister Meemaw," she said. "But I couldn't eat it either." As we followed the nuns into the park, Honey threw the mint into a hedge sculpted in the shape of a fox.

Salvia waited for us on the other side of the turnstiles. "Do you know Pinocchio?" she asked us.

Honey began to hum *When You Wish Upon a Star*.

Salvia laughed. "I have seen this movie," she said. "It is not exactly the story. Pinocchio is a boy made of wood and he tries so hard to be good, but he is *birichino*. A mischief. And he is not obeying his father even though he loves him. He is tricked by the bad fox and cat. And he is swallowed by *Il Terribile Pescecane*."

"The whale?"

Salvia waggled her fingers. "You will see. And the Blue Fairy rescues him and his father too and he becomes a real boy."

Ahead of Salvia, I saw the elderly nun she usually walked with.

"I help Suor Cristina," she said. "We are here until fifteen-thirty."

Honey and I ventured into the park together.

"This is even stranger than the game shows," Honey said, eyebrows raised.

We began noticing the nuns—our nuns—in different places around the park, at tables in the shade, playing chess on a giant chess board. Some had brought books to read. We saw one nun sitting with her face to the sun, tanning. We did not see any of the nuns riding on the carousel or the small zipline across the river, but we did see several sitting at the puppet show.

Honey was amused by it, but there was something about it that made me feel heavy. I had enjoyed the ride with Salvia, but the pond and the maze increasingly reminded me of the garden we visited with the boys. It gave me a feeling of nostalgia, of homesickness, of wishing for times past when we were all under one roof, when we were on holidays together. Then I saw a young father holding a baby.

I wondered whether Honey would mind if I left her, but she wanted me to take pictures of her on her phone, pictures she posted instantly on Instagram.

We reached the far end of the park. Ahead of us was a large Plexiglass form, half-submerged in the water of the pond. It was a whale—or as the English version of the sign called it, The Terrible Dogfish. It had rows of teeth sticking out, large white wooden teeth, as unscary as those of the fake shark in *Jaws*.

There was a large pink inflated couch in the center of the Terrible Dogfish, what I realized was supposed to be the tongue of the beast. A family was seated on the tongue as we arrived, but when they saw us, they left, and Honey flopped down on it. I joined her.

"So, you really only have a couple weeks left?" I said to fill the silence. "What's next for you?"

Honey sighed and lay back on the inflated tongue, looking at her newly painted fingernails. "I don't know," she said. "My cousin is getting married in June and my mother is hosting The Biggest Wedding Shower of All Time, and she's been begging me to come back. And she's running for re-election this fall in the state legislature, and she'd like me to help with her campaign."

"And?"

She frowned. "And the last time around, she kind of wanted me to hide. At least that's how I read it. She wanted me to wear long sleeves and hide my tattoos."

"And this time?"

"I don't know. I kind of want to go. But I don't want her to squash me either, to make me be her arm-candy, her perfect daughter."

"It's hard," I said. I knew hard.

"I miss my little brother, too," she said. "I've been thinking maybe he'd like me to read *Charlotte's Web* out loud to him. Or even just the whole of *Goodnight Moon*. You know?"

"I didn't know you had a little brother."

"Jake's nine. They gave him a phone for Christmas and he's been texting me every day since then."

"Sounds like you're going back," I said. "And who knows, maybe your mom will surprise you." It felt like a bit of an out-of-body experience to hear myself say those words. To think about mothers who surprised their children, children who surprised their mothers.

"You sound tired," Honey said. "Or sad. Are you feeling okay?"

I kept thinking about my children and I sat quietly until I could contain myself no longer. I took a deep breath. "Can I ask you a personal question?" I asked her.

"Sure."

"What do you think about abortion?"

Honey cocked her head toward me as if evaluating whether I was asking for myself—and it wasn't an utter impossibility.

"It's super-sad," she said, cautiously. "A kind of last option. Why?"

I had skirted the issue long enough. There, in the mouth of the Terrible Dogfish, in the world's strangest theme park, I finally found the courage to begin to speak about what had brought me to Italy, to say the words aloud for the very first time: "My son had an abortion. I mean, my son's girlfriend."

Jackson's girlfriend, Caitlin. But he went with her to the clinic at the hospital, in their university town. He held her hand and, as I was told much later, apparently brought her a smoothie afterwards.

"And that's not a choice you supported?" Honey said, her face clouded, her voice tight.

People always assigned me a side, always assumed I held a simple and hateful position, but this took away my choice to show where I stood. I knew what it was to hold unbearable, impossible tensions. I suddenly understood the astronomer's tee shirt, the cats that were both alive and dead simultaneously.

"It wasn't just an abortion," I said. "It's not that simple."

There were so many layers to this situation before you got to where it was tragic. And it had been hard enough for me to say this much to Honey. But just as empty nest syndrome had been too trite an explanation for my grief, so summing it up as being against someone choosing to have an abortion was inflammatory, wrong. Sitting among the teeth of the Terrible Dogfish, listening to Honey's story about her mom, I knew there were many different ways to tell the same story. And sometimes you couldn't tell your version of the story. Not yet.

I also saw that Honey's simple answer was the truth. Regardless of what I or anyone thought or did, most people would agree that something about abortion was super-sad.

"Do you think . . . ?" I began, but then I couldn't finish the sentence aloud even though I knew what I wanted to say: *Do you think I should have done something differently?* "Do you think they're sad?" I asked finally.

24

It was Joanna who gave the secret away at the ladies retreat in the middle of October. She invited me to walk the labyrinth at the retreat center with her, but I soon realized that it was more of an excuse to talk to me on our own. The sign outside the labyrinth said a maze was not a labyrinth, that you would find your way through if you followed the path. It also said people walking the labyrinth were to walk in silence. I followed Joanna, stepping single file between the fieldstones that were arranged in circles.

"How's Jackson doing?" she asked meaningfully.

There was no one else around we would disturb with our conversation. "He's good, I think," I said, shrugging my shoulders. "We talk or text with all of them every few days. He's good. They all are. How's Jess doing at school?"

"No, I mean how is he *really* doing?"

I stopped at the turning between one circle and another to face her. "What do you mean?"

"I mean, the baby and all. Chrissy said Caitlin is fine but they broke up and I just wondered how Jackson was taking it."

I stared at her. "I don't know what you're talking about," I said. Joanna knew that I knew about the breakup. It was the part before that.

She sighed. "Look, fine. I know it's awkward and awful, and you can just say so if you don't want to talk about it."

"I don't want to talk about it," I said. The sign had said if you stayed between the stone markers and followed the path, everything would lead to the center and back out again, but I suddenly felt trapped by the path that lay open before and behind me. Without thinking, I stepped over four rows of stones and back out to the main path, leaving Joanna behind, shocked that I would violate a labyrinth, and me not caring.

On my way to the main lodge again, I pulled my phone out of my pocket. There was no cell reception. I found a higher point on the property, a place where an enormous wooden cross had been erected, and there I found I had two bars on my phone. I dialed Russ's number.

"What baby?" I said when he answered.

"Liz?" he said.

"Of course it's me," I said. "What is Joanna talking about, about Jackson and Caitlin and a baby?"

"Oh," he said, and I knew from his voice that he knew.

"When?" I asked.

"In the spring," he said.

I swallowed hard. *When were you going to tell me?* The question was on the tip of my tongue to ask and then I realized: he wasn't. No one was going to tell me. It was the myth they all believed: that you could erase someone. Not only had a baby—*a baby!*—been erased, but so had I. I had been erased from mattering, from having a voice, from being a grandmother or even a mother. I felt forsaken. Forsaken and shaken.

I hung up the phone. I had never hung up on Russ before.

I couldn't stay at the retreat for the night. I knew that. I caught up to Joanna who was returning from the labyrinth.

"I'm not ready to talk about it," I said again, using the words she had given me. "I have to go home. Please don't, don't say—"

"Of course I won't say anything," she said. "Of course it's raw for you still. I should have let you bring it up in your own time."

"Thank you," I said. I could trust her not to say anything. I knew that. She was a true friend. But I could not trust her enough, not then anyhow, to tell her that she had told me something I had not known. I had known her for more than twenty years. She had a daughter a year younger than Jackson and one Gil's age. We had joked before about our kids marrying.

I went into the lodge where the session had begun again, and there was a worship band at the front, with a synthesizer and a woman who had entirely too much of what my mother would call *pep* leading the group in song. I could not flee quickly enough.

I packed my bags and loaded my car. Joanna had said she would explain that I had to leave without getting into details. When I got into my car, I did not know where to go. Could I go home?

25

I HADN'T THOUGHT MUCH ABOUT MARY BEFORE I came to Italy. In my church growing up, Mary made an annual appearance in the children's Nativity play, and her costume was a beautiful silky blue robe, so that every girl wanted to be her. The angels were the only other girl part but their costumes were heavy and the wings were dusty and fragile. Not only did Mary get the better costume but she also got to hold the real baby Jesus—our church's tradition was that one of the youngest members of the church would be recruited to be wrapped in a towel and laid in a wooden box. I got to be Mary once when I was nine or ten. I expected to feel like a celebrity, but it was a surprisingly meaningful and moving experience for me, and the baby who was my Jesus, Jason Ward, grew up into a boy I always felt a special care for.

That was my sole experience with Mary until I shared a room with a large portrait of her. *Our Lady of Perpetual Constipation*, Cecy had nicknamed the painting, and I had made my own jokes about it, calling her my roommate in my emails to Russ and Karin and Joanna.

But something stopped feeling jokey in me when I visited the Duomo Museum the Saturday after our trip to the Pinocchio Park. There I learned that the story of the church built without a roof was true. I looked at the relic of John the Baptist's finger and the glorious original Brunelleschi doors. Then, in a quiet alcove, crisscrossed by a laser security system, I saw a statue made of four figures. I had no idea who two of the figures were, but I knew the others in a heartbeat: Mary, holding up the body of her dead son, Jesus. His head had fallen against her forehead, and his body leaned against hers, a grown man, a dead man, in the posture of a sleepy toddler, while her hand held him from falling.

There was a bench right across from the statue, a bench in the shadows, and I was grateful for it, sinking onto it with a sense of recognition and sympathy that made my legs feel weak beneath me.

I accidentally activated the alarm twice, simply by leaning forward to look more closely at the sculpture. The security guard who came to check didn't look the least bit suspicious that I might have done anything untoward—clearly false alarms happened all the time.

Although I eventually moved on to see the rest of the museum, it was the statue—the *Pietà*—I thought of when I returned to my room. I hadn't touched the statue but now I put a hand on the frame of the painting in my room.

"You lost your son," I said quietly. "Me too."

Obviously Jackson had not been put to a violent death or anything, but there was something deeply painful in having a son who was unwilling to turn to me, and who made choices that grieved my heart.

I saw beyond the painting of Mary to its deeper meaning. I had walked through the empty bedrooms in our little Lemonland apartment and had seen the woman in white in Cecy's old room. I had to admit that Cecy had a point in naming it *Of Course I'm A Virgin, How Dare You. Jesus, Bloody Jesus* in Honey's room showed fat drops of blood oozing down Jesus's face from a crown of thorns, while the fourth room had a large painting of a bearded old man in a crown, finger upraised, with two small figures above him. I had no idea who it was supposed to be. Even though my painting of Mary wasn't especially artistic, it showed me a kindred spirit.

I sat down, cross-legged, on my bed.

"So," I said to Mary. I had said it to Honey the week before and now I said the words again. "So my son had an abortion and that's why I'm here."

I paused. What was I expecting? I was not accustomed to audible answers to prayer and I didn't expect an answer from a painting. I thought of what Salvia had said about the Blue Fairy rescuing Pinocchio, but I had enough fear instilled in me by my religiously conservative mother that I knew I was not praying to Mary even if she was dressed in blue.

It was just that it seemed like a safe place to say some of what I had to say, safe in a way that talking to friends wasn't, in a way that journaling hadn't been, let alone praying.

I thought of my desire to be mothered, to be sheltered in my mother's lap. I thought of the *Pietà*, of Mary holding the dead Jesus in her lap. She was safe partly because I was fairly sure she couldn't actually hear me, but also because I felt like Mary's real experience was one that made her someone I would like to talk to, like an old friend, like a mother. Maybe I could find the words by talking to her.

26

I ONCE WENT TO A FUNERAL OF A BABY. THE COFFIN was white and small enough to sit on a small table, light enough to be carried by one person. As for Jackson's baby, I knew that the hospital would have disposed of the remains, along with removed gall bladders, appendixes, tumors. There would have been nothing to bury. I did not even know when the baby had been due, how quickly they had made the decision.

Although I didn't tell anyone, I held my own funeral for the baby. In late November, before the ground froze solid, I went to the hardware store and chose a bag full of tiny brown knots, bulbs. Below the picture on the packet of scilla bulbs, it said they would naturalize and spread, that they would come up early in the spring. It said they looked like stars. I liked the thought that they would come up year after year, a memorial to the child who had been real, who had had a beating heart, who had been unnamed. As I planted the bulbs, I mouthed two names—just to name her or him. I doubted that Caitlin or Jackson had named it—although who knew—but I named the baby, saying the names silently as I planted the bulbs and hoped they would grow.

27

The day after I talked with Mary about my troubles, I didn't even ask myself if I wanted to go to the English Church. Instead I slept in and then went to visit the Leonardo da Vinci Museum.

I was on the bus back to the convent in the late afternoon when suddenly I knew that I was being watched. I found my senses bristling, my awareness heightened. I was many stops away from mine, and from there, I would have the ten-minute walk up the hill, past enormous houses in front of which I had only ever seen the occasional gardener as a sign of human life. I could not count on help from any of those houses, and it would only be once I got within the safe confines of the gated convent that I would be able to breathe again.

If the staring continued, I would take the bus straight to the Piazzale Michelangelo, I decided. It was always filled with tourists, night and day, and I could likely find an English-speaking tourist there to whom I could explain my situation.

A hand wrapped around my arm. I gasped. My heart began to race. Here it was at last.

I looked at the hand and then down into the face of a young boy, his hand on my arm, his expression curious.

"*Occhi blu*," he said, looking up at me in wonder. He touched the corner of his eyes and then pointed up at my face. "*Occhi blu*." My blue eyes had caught his attention. I realized what made his own eyes distinctive: he had Down syndrome.

"*Sì*," I managed to say.

"*Bella signora*," he said, and then his mother, I presumed, saw what he was doing and pulled him away from me, explaining in earnest but exasperated Italian a lesson I assumed meant he shouldn't bother me.

"*Scusi,*" she said to me.

"*Scusi,*" he echoed.

My limbs felt weak with fear dissipating, but I smiled with the sisterhood of mothers, the understanding of what children are like.

I thought of the whistle I wore under my clothes like an amulet of protection every time I left the safety of the convent gates. I looked over at the boy who was now seated on his mother's lap, patting her face. I reached under my shirt for the whistle on its brown leather cord and held it in my hand.

I stayed on the bus past my stop, past the stop where the boy and his mother disembarked, waving back at them as they began making their way along the sidewalk. I wasn't sure why I stayed on the bus until I stood up to get off at the exit nearest San Miniato. I mounted the dozens of stairs to the church, stretching out muscles that had cramped tight as I bent and reached to prune trees, and as I had tightened in fear on the bus.

As I entered the building in the late afternoon light, I could hear from the absence of song that Sunday evening Vespers had not yet begun. I followed the sound of voices down to what I had come to realize was a crypt, the whistle still in my hand. I had never blown it. I didn't know how shrill it would be, how effective.

I took a seat on the wooden benches, and exhaled, feeling again the small hand on my arm, my terror, my relief. Over the weeks, I had moved up from my initial seat on the cold marble steps to sit on the benches.

Behind me two women were talking, their voices quiet but echoing off the vaulted ceiling. I had seen them before, and they smiled at me as I came in, making me wonder whether perhaps I was part of a church community of sorts. Now I was surprised when I could comprehend what they were saying and then I realized it was because they were speaking English.

They were talking about a group that met at San Miniato, a grief group. One of the women had been part of it after her husband died and she was encouraging the other woman to join. The second woman wasn't sure. "I'm doing fine," she said.

I wondered, as the monks took their places behind the screen, whether I could say the same. I wondered whether I could join a grief group. Then the monks began to sing and the music washed over me, and I felt comfort being hidden deep within this church, recognizing why I had stayed on the bus, to return to this place of hiddenness as though it were a womb.

I had no idea what the monks sang, other than the occasional word that resembled the English version, but the practice of sitting quietly was a new one for me, a good one. I thought about how I had long been busy and anxious about so many things.

I watched as the monk who was leading communion that day placed wafers in the mouths of those who lined up in front of him, including the two women who had sat behind me. I twisted the whistle's cord in my lap.

I wondered what the boy on the bus would have done if I had blown my whistle. I wondered what loveliness I had missed by traveling with it at the ready. Now that I had spoken about Jackson and the baby, my general sense of danger had subsided. I imagined dropping the whistle into the Arno or leaving it in my room at the convent.

As I left the church after the Vespers service I passed a pile of crutches, eyeglasses, hearing aids, and wheelchairs just inside the door. I had seen such piles in various Italian churches, devices abandoned as signs of healing, as proof that they were no longer needed. Without thinking about it, I turned, tucked my whistle into the pile at the door to San Miniato and stepped out into the navy-blue sky of early evening, feeling oddly naked, but somehow free. Descending into the piazza, I spotted the bitter woman from the *tabacchi*. She was sucking on a cigarette, blowing smoke from the slash that had become her mouth, and I was tempted to wave, so light was my mood.

When I got back to Lemonland, Honey was on the couch in the common room.

"You'll never guess what I did today," I said, hoping Honey wouldn't think I had been ridiculous either to bring the whistle to Italy in the first place or to toss it.

Honey moved to the end of the couch, making a place for me to sit.

"I threw away my security whistle," I said.

She gestured and I handed my feet into her lap. As she kneaded my feet, I told her the story about the whistle and then everything I'd said to the portrait of Mary, and the knots began to slip away.

28

When I was a little girl, I watched *The Flintstones* every single day at lunch, while I ate whatever my mother had made—Kraft Dinner or grilled cheese sandwiches or Campbell's soup—on a television tray in front of Fred and Wilma. There was one episode that gave me bad dreams, a James Bond-like episode with a villain called Dr. Sinister whose lair included a bottomless pit. Dr. Sinister would throw a rock into the pit, and Fred and Barney would listen and hear nothing because the pit was bottomless.

We just keep falling? Fred says.

That's right, Dr. Sinister replies. *Forever and ever and ever.*

The thought of falling forever and ever was terrifying, and I thought of that episode in my second pregnancy, the pregnancy where the ultrasound technician couldn't find a heartbeat, where the doctor induced labor, where grief laid me low.

My fear was that the grief would go on forever and ever and ever, and the miracle was that as sad as this miscarriage was, the grief was *not* bottomless. There was Timothy who brought me his sippy cup to share, and Russ who brought me coffee and wine and seafood, all the things I had abstained from to protect the baby from harm. Joanna made supper for our family as I lay in bed, weary and worn.

I hadn't been able to protect the baby but the doctor told me, "There's nothing you could have done. There's nothing you did to cause this and nothing that would have prevented it." That too was grace.

When I got pregnant again with Jackson a few months later, at first I was cautious about every twinge and I was scared to enter into the joy of it, but then one day, playing with Timothy and Russ at the park, I realized that this child was a gift, mine to love for as long as he lived inside me or outside me. He wasn't mine to wrap in bubble wrap. I couldn't protect him from all pain. I learned that before Jackson was even born. I had had innocent joy in mothering Timothy. After the miscarriage that innocence turned into something more real, a scarred but deeper joy.

29

I WONDERED WHAT WE WOULD DO ONCE THE TREES were pruned, but on the day we finished our last tree, Niccolò told us our next task was to fertilize the trees before it got too hot. Honey knew what this was about and she rolled her eyes.

"On one of our first days here, back in January," she explained to me, "This old guy showed up with a tiny tractor pulling a long narrow wagon. It was piled high with horseshit. I mean that literally."

They had apparently dumped what was called green manure, the droppings of grass-fed horses, in a pile beyond the *glicine*, far from the convent house.

"For the first time, I'm wishing I had booked my ticket home for sooner," she said. "Niccolò said it had to sit all winter. I figured I'd be gone before it had to be dealt with."

I had worked well-rotted manure into my garden last fall, feeling it was an appropriate medium in which to work; I knew from that experience that it would have no smell at all. Honey was dubious, and reluctant to get involved in what she called "a really crappy job." I agreed to shovel the manure into and out of the wheelbarrow, and she would push the wheelbarrow around the trees. I told her that we were a different kind of mud angels, and I explained about the flood of 1966.

As we went, I smelled lilacs in bloom around the convent property, a flower I always associated with Mother's Day at home. It disoriented me to be in full warm spring in March.

By noon it turned really hot and Niccolò told us we would take the whole afternoon off. I wondered how warm he must be in his cassock, thought of jokes Cecy would make about kilts, and smothered the thought.

Honey and I trudged back upstairs to Lemonland, where I let her shower first. When I came out of the tiny bathroom, mercifully clean and cool, Honey was standing across from the doorway in a dress, a bottle in each hand and a striped beach towel slung around her neck.

"I've got an idea," she said with a grin.

Her idea, it turned out, was to even out her farmer's tan before she went home. One of the bottles was sunscreen and the other was limoncello.

"I didn't bring a bathing suit with me," I said.

She shrugged. "Just wear your bra and panties. No one will come looking for us. They'll be at their prayers."

It was true—we often heard the nuns singing their prayers on warm afternoons when they opened the windows of the chapel to allow in a breeze.

"What about the guests?" I said. A trio of nuns from a different convent had arrived the night before and a honey-mooning couple was staying there for the week.

"They're probably either naked themselves or have better things to do."

I must have hesitated slightly because Honey thrust the limoncello at me. The bottle was icy cold and beaded with condensation. I took a whiff: it smelled tart and sweet and strong. I laughed. "Why not?"

I put on fresh clothes and took my damp towel from the bathroom. In the heat it would dry quickly.

We snuck down the outside metal stairs near the *limonaia* from which the scent of citrus blossoms rose in the heat as heavy and decadent as incense.

"Where?" Honey asked as we reached the terrace. "Not near the manure."

I thought for a moment and remembered the circle of cypresses I had found on my first day at the convent. Wrapping the bottle of limoncello in my towel, I pointed in the direction of the cypresses and led the way. We stepped into shade as dark as the trees that made it and we were in the clear. I stopped and laughed, feeling conspiratorial as if we were playing hooky.

We walked down the stairs that were big enough for giants.

"You know the story of this place?" Honey asked, pointing farther down the steps to the bottom of the property. "The girl who was here when I got here told me the story. Apparently this wasn't always a convent. It was built by a friend of Galileo's and then it was passed down through the family until the last owner died in the '70s, leaving it to the nuns."

"I heard about Galileo," I said, remembering the scientist in the cat tee shirt who had told me the story.

"That isn't even the best part. Apparently in the late '30s or early '40s, before the war started, Hitler came to visit Mussolini and they drove up into the hills and right along the road below the property. Everyone came out to watch as they drove by.

"And—" Honey stopped and put a hand on my arm—"the woman who owned this villa came down here with a friend to watch them drive by, and she turned to her friend and said, 'Imagine, darling, if only we had a bomb.'"

Honey laughed and skipped ahead, twirling her towel. "Imagine, darling," she said.

"Back here," I called. It was the path that led to the cypress grove.

She came back up the stairs and we found the grassy space and somehow the angle of the sun was just right.

"Awesome-issimo," she said. "This is perfect." She spread her towel on the ground and pulled her phone out of the pocket of her dress. "Will it bug you if I play music?"

"As long as the nuns don't hear it and come to investigate, I don't mind." I didn't think they could hear us. We were far enough away from the house.

I spread out my towel, checking the ground carefully first. I had seen a number of tiny green lizards sunning themselves as we pruned. They were the size of grasshoppers so they barely startled me, but I had read that there were vipers in Tuscany so I looked before I sat down.

Honey pulled her dress over her head to reveal red bikini bottoms and nothing else.

"When in Rome," she said with a laugh, as she rolled up her dress to make a pillow, and then began carefully applying sunscreen only to the parts of her that were already tanned, her forearms, knees and the back of her neck. "Do you know what Italians call pasty white people like us? Mozzarella! That's what people in my running group say."

She settled herself down on her towel, turned her music on, and closed her eyes.

"Limoncello?" I offered, and without opening her eyes, she raised one hand for the bottle.

After she drank some, she passed it back to me and I took a long drink. It was icy cold and sour and sweet, and I laughed out loud at the intensity of it.

Honey looked over at me. "Italy's been good for you, hasn't it? I mean, it's been good for me too, but you threw away your whistle and now you're slugging limoncello."

I laughed again and put the bottle halfway between us. Honey took another drink and closed her eyes again. I took off my shorts and my shirt, and folded them up to make a pillow.

I reached for the sunscreen and began covering myself. There were parts of my skin—my belly, for instance—that hadn't seen sunlight since the '80s. Mozzarella, indeed.

As I lay back and closed my eyes, at first I felt exposed with my hair cut off and my clothes largely removed in a semi-public place. But the warm gaze of the sun and the remembrance of all the naked bodies sculpted in stone I had seen in museums and piazzas—the *Davids*, for instance—soon softened my shyness. I lay still for a few minutes and then I undid my own bra and put it beside me.

I had it on again before Honey turned over to bake the other side of her, but it was enough. I hadn't removed it to keep up with her, or to pretend I had no inhibitions. I had simply wanted to know what it was to be naked and unashamed in a garden.

When we went back up to our rooms an hour and a half later, I showered again. I could feel the slightest sunburn despite the weak spring sun. There had been a time when my breasts were regularly exposed, during the years I nursed the boys. It had been a satisfaction to nourish them. And, of course, I had been naked in intimacy with Ross. But this was the first time I had ever felt the pure pleasure of having a warm breeze on my naked skin. It had been a circle of protection, not a dead end, the clearing among the cypresses.

"Imagine, darling, if only we had a bomb," I said to myself, as the water of the shower fell over me like warm spring sunlight on bare skin.

30

THE MOST AWKWARD CONVERSATION IN PARENTING is nearly always the one about the birds and the bees. It's a conversation where eye contact is avoided. It's a conversation with implications about both the parent and child's behavior, potentially revealing knowledge that could make both feel very uncomfortable.

I had talked with the boys when they were young, about body parts and respect, but I had left The Talk to Russ, equipping him with books and movies he could use. I'd had conversations about relationships with the boys over the years, but as much as I was comfortable talking about sex, I'd opted out of any frank conversation with my own sons, just as my own parents had, something I grieved as I pulled dead plants from my garden last fall.

When I found out about Jackson, anything I could think of to say sounded like those awkward conversations. Of course they were intimate. They didn't live together, although they had traveled together. But the fact that there had been consequences made me feel like there was no way I could talk with him about it without sounding judgmental or punitive.

I could respect their choices, even if they weren't the choices I might make. But I couldn't find the skills I usually brought to this conversation. Instead I felt such a ball of emotions that I spent hours trying to untangle them. I felt angry at myself: I had always hoped and believed I would be generous enough to support a child of mine in their choices, but this particular question had always seemed theoretical as I had no daughters. This business with Jackson caught me so unprepared and showed me how conflicted I really was.

Anything I could think of to say sounded defensive and condemning. In my nights of staring at the ceiling, I realized that I judged myself for this as much as I judged them.

But I could deal with my feelings and my judgment. What was worse was betrayal. That Jackson had told Russ and maybe Tim and Gil, and that Joanna knew, but not me. It stung with a sense of profound rejection. I had been left out of the conversation—no one had had The Talk with me.

31

Two days later, as we headed out to the olive grove, the nun with the beetle eyebrows stood in the doorway to stop me. I wasn't sure which nun was the Mother Superior or equivalent, but she was one of my guesses.

"Elizabetta," she said to me. "*Vieni nel mio ufficio*."

Salvia stood nearby, staring down at the floor. "*Madre* Maria-Caterina wants you to come to her office." I had guessed right but now I felt like I was being called in before the principal.

"Me too?" Honey asked.

The Mother Superior shook her head fiercely and pointed in the direction of the olive grove. Honey threw me a look and headed outside. I followed the *Madre* and Salvia, not to the main office but to a small room with a large wooden desk. Behind the desk was a large crucifix with Jesus twisting in agony on it.

The Mother Superior sat behind her desk and motioned for me to sit in one of the chairs in front of it. I did, expecting Salvia to take the other. Instead Salvia stood behind the desk, within arm's reach of the woman who was clearly in charge.

The Mother Superior gathered her brows like a storm cloud and began to speak quietly but firmly. I had no idea what she was saying. I looked at Salvia for help, but she was watching the Mother Superior, listening carefully. The older woman stopped speaking and looked sternly at Salvia.

Salvia spoke so quietly I had to lean forward to hear her. "*Madre* asks me to do the translation of her words. She appreciate you are a good worker and a pleasant guest. You do not stay out at night or cause any disasters."

The Mother Superior held up a cautionary finger and gave another long speech.

"However," Salvia said, looking smaller than ever, "she is concern you ask the personal questions about the *suore* before we come here. About our families. She does not wish for the *suore* to be distracted from the vocation."

The Mother Superior spoke again, briefly, looked at Salvia, and then stood up.

"She is certain you mean no harm, but she ask you to respect the vows we take."

My cheeks burned. The Mother Superior would make a lousy customs agent, I thought. But I knew, from my Italian classes, what to say when you had offended someone, and I said it. "*Mi dispiace.*"

The Mother Superior nodded and remained standing. Salvia led me out of the room.

"I'm so sorry," I said to Salvia. She smiled, briefly, not angry, and then she scuttled off, leaving me to find my own way to the olive grove.

I found Honey who was waiting on the terrace. "What was that all about?" she asked. "Are we in trouble for sunbathing?"

As I opened my mouth to speak, I felt an incredible wave of shame and anger. "I'm in trouble for talking with Salvia about her family, for distracting her from her vocation."

It felt unfair, not only to me but to Salvia, to put her in an awkward position of having to translate something we all knew was about her. I hadn't asked Salvia if she hated being a nun. I hadn't done anything wrong, and yet the Mother Superior had yelled at me. Or at least it felt like she had.

"Good Lord," Honey said. "She needs to get laid. Oh wait, that's me. No, seriously, Liz, don't let it bug you. You didn't do anything wrong."

I *was* bugged. We were on our very last row of fertilizing the trees. We had seen bonfires from around the valley—other olive groves that had finished pruning their trees—burning the branches. The pile in the firepit was huge now. We were going to light it that afternoon. I hadn't done anything wrong—as far as I could tell—and yet I was in trouble.

As the morning wore on, even as I dumped great piles of manure around the bases of trees, I continued to feel heavy. When we stopped for lunch, I almost felt ashamed about going inside for lunch. Should I talk with Salvia? Would the Mother Superior be watching me?

The *Madre* was the one to bring us a bean-tomato-sage stew, followed by the very elderly nun carrying us a basket of bread. As had happened before, the *Madre* hurried back to the kitchen, letting the door swing heavily, nearly crashing into the elderly nun. I jumped up from my table and held the door open for her, daring the Mother Superior to take me aside again.

As I lay on my bed that afternoon, I wondered why I was so upset. It was more than just being shamed for being kind. It was also related to the interaction between the nuns at lunch. Somehow I had idealized the nuns. I had seen them walk in their two lines as though they were cute little figures, as though they were caricatures, my fantasy of an idealized community. I had come to them as a safe place, and I had imagined that meant they were perfect. I didn't know what to do when they weren't.

We had spent weeks filling the pit with branches, and now Niccolò had us don long thick gloves to pull out half of the branches onto the tarp and to drag it some distance from the pit. We would add wood to the fire throughout the afternoon as it burned down, but he did not want to create a massive bonfire that might injure us or the *glicine*—which had begun to sprout green buds all over it, proving it wasn't dead.

We sat all afternoon on stools Niccolò brought over for us, feeding sticks into the fire. It made me think of spring nights with my father, making maple syrup over a woodstove in our backyard. As the afternoon and the fire burned on, Niccolò told us that he had tended this grove from the time the convent moved into the villa. When the Sisters of Stability and Charity had arrived, he said, the gardens were well-tended but the olive grove was completely overgrown. Some of the trees, he said, had not been pruned in a hundred years. He recalled how he found one tree, still alive, buried beneath the branches of three other trees that interlocked over the top of them. He laced his fingers to show us what he meant.

I wondered whether the Mother Superior was watching from the house, whether she worried I was leading Niccolò astray as I had apparently led Salvia. I sat quietly, the flames warming my face, listening to his stories.

He told us he had been chosen to come to help out because he was a strong teenager, a novice in his monastery, and because he had been raised on a farm. But his family's farm hadn't grown olives and he hadn't known what to do. It was the first Mother Superior, *Madre* Carmela, *pace all'anima sua*, who taught him what he needed to know. It was not until five years later, he told us with a wheezing laugh, that the Mother Superior confessed she had learned how to prune the trees from a book at the library.

"But it worked," Niccolò said. "She always says she has to do whatever she can."

I tilted my head like the picture of Mary in my room. I understood the impulse of a mother, even a mother of a flock of nuns, to do whatever it took to care for and protect her flock. I supposed that was what *Madre* Maria-Catarina was doing, whatever she had to do.

I hadn't done anything wrong. I hadn't led Salvia astray—at least I was fairly sure I hadn't. I wondered whether the Mother Superior had been sitting behind us on the bus to the Pinocchio Park, or perhaps whether Salvia had confessed our conversations to her. Maybe my innocent questions had caused Salvia to rethink her choices. I had begun to read a copy of *Pinocchio* I had picked up in the bookstore at the theme park, and now I wondered if I was like that boy, meaning well but easily straying.

Maybe it was simply a clash of values with the Mother Superior. Or maybe I had treated the nuns as though they were there for my sake, my interest, and my comfort, rather than respecting their hospitality.

We stayed outside all afternoon, feeding the fire until the branches were all ashes. The smoke from the fire was fragrant and dark, and I watched it rise up into the blue sky and I thought about everything that had brought me to this place.

32

I GREW UP IN SUBURBAN WATERLOO WHERE PEOPLE just didn't do this kind of thing but we had four large sugar maples in our yard, and for as long as I could remember, my father tapped the trees every year and made maple syrup. My mother made him tap the side of the trees that faced the house rather than the street because she didn't want people to see what he was doing. It took forty litres of sap to make one litre of syrup, I remember.

Every day after school in late February and through March I would check the buckets to see how much sap had flowed that day. I remember the pride I felt when my dad decided I was old enough to be trusted to carry buckets of the precious sap to the garage where he stored the sap, covered. Every Friday night in maple season, he would build a fire in the cookstove he'd built in our backyard for this purpose. He burned applewood he bought from Mennonite farmers after he heard that apple was the hardest, best-smelling wood to burn when making syrup. He poured buckets of sap into a large kettle that sat above the fire and he stirred it occasionally in the first few hours, and then constantly as it got closer to turning into syrup. The first batch usually was close to ready sometime late on Saturday night or early Sunday morning. I would hear him slip out of the house to check on the syrup once or twice on Friday nights but he stayed up all night Saturday night with the syrup, until it was done. As I got older, I was allowed to sit up with him.

One year, we made syrup on the night before Easter, and the night was warm. My dad pulled out lawn chairs and made us hot tea. We wrapped ourselves in blankets and sat and talked until well into the night. At some point I must have dozed off because the next thing I remembered was my dad waking me up. It was just before sunrise, and the sky was still dark.

"Happy Easter, kiddo," he said, and he handed me a little bowl of maple syrup, still warm, and a spoon.

We named Jackson after him because he died the summer before Jackson was born. He was quiet and complicated and he made the sweetest maple syrup.

33

THE DAY STARTED OUT WITH PROMISE. Elora and Patrizia picked me up right at the convent the following weekend and although I was squashed sideways in the backseat of the car, it was warm enough to open the windows as we drove up the *autostrada*. Neither Patrizia nor Elora wore seatbelts which worried me, especially as we were so soon into the mountains. I consoled myself with the thought that the way the car was built there was no physical way either of them could land on me in the event of any kind of crash—but I kept wanting to tell them to put their seatbelts on, like I was their mother.

They spoke to one another in a familiar Italian-English mix over the sound of the motor and the wind and the rush of traffic.

As she drove, Patrizia told a story about an elderly customer the day before who had paid for her wash and set in advance, because she was afraid she would forget to pay at the end—and then paid again when it was done, having forgotten she had paid beforehand. When they both laughed, I thought of the characters of Fox and Cat in the story of *Pinocchio*, the tricksters who had successfully persuaded Pinocchio to believe in the Field of Dreams, who had told him if he planted his gold coins there, a money tree would grow, and he could give even more money to his poor father. Elora and Patrizia both laughed, and I cringed in the backseat.

But there was a saying we used in my work, used often in fact: "Not my circus, not my monkeys." It was all too easy to try to fix people, to know what they ought to do, to be moved by compassion that slid so easily into control. At work it became shorthand for establishing boundaries. How Patrizia conducted her business was not my circus or my monkeys.

I looked out the window instead. I could feel, even more than see, how we were wending our way higher into the mountains. The sky was a brilliant blue.

When Patrizia pulled off the *autostrada* to fill the tank, I handed her a rolled-up wad of euros for gas money. "*Grazie*," she said.

"Need to pee?" Elora asked me.

I wasn't sure I would be able to get myself back into the backseat of the car without a crowbar so I declined. Elora crawled out and stretched in the sunshine like a dancer while Patrizia stood at the pump and filled the car with gas. Then Elora went into the *autogrill.*

When Elora returned, she carried a cardboard tray that looked something like a Tim Hortons takeout tray in Canada, but instead of double-doubles, the tray held three plastic glasses filled with a purplish-red liquid.

"*Spremuta*," she explained, handing me one. "Orange juice. Blood oranges."

I took a cautious sip and it was delicious. A less acidic, softer orange juice. I asked her the Italian word again as Patrizia got back into the car.

"We always asked our papa to stop along the highway for *spremuta*," Patrizia said. "It sounded so exotic, so exciting. He always said it is too expensive, but one day he agreed and bought us some, my sister and me. And we were so disappointed because it was the same as the juice we made at home from oranges."

She swerved onto the highway and the road continued uphill into the mountains. Elora turned on the radio to a kind of music that sounded like every song on the Italian gameshows, and she called out cities and towns to me—Prato, Vergato, Bologna, Sassuolo, Reggio Emilia—over the sound of the music and the wind blowing in her window.

Then ahead of us the mountains abruptly came to an end, and stretching out ahead of us was a vast plain, a flat area. As we descended into it, my ears popped.

"We are almost there," Patrizia said. "Shall we stop for lunch?"

It was another twenty minutes before she stopped, twenty minutes of driving along the flat highway and then turning back toward the mountains. She came to a little town in the foothills, and slowed down, evaluating this café and that restaurant before finally pulling over at a small parking lot which housed a food truck in the corner. As we got out of the car and my legs were able to bend again—thinking the phrase "deep vein thrombosis" and realizing that airlines could squeeze people in even more tightly than they did—my nose caught the smell of what I recognized as basil and tomatoes.

We sat at a small picnic table next to the food truck. While we ate an enormously large pizza, splotched with white rounds of mozzarella and still-green basil leaves and drizzled with olive oil, Elora moved into tourist-guide mode, even without her peacock feather.

"This is where Patrizia grew up," Elora said. "And the castles we are going to see were built nearly a thousand years ago by the most famous woman leader in the Middle Ages, Mathilda of Canossa. Have you ever heard of her?"

I had not. Mathilda, Elora explained, had built a range of castles along the edge of the mountains, facing out into the plain, to defend her territory. And she had done so ably.

When we got back into the car, Elora insisted I sit in the front seat so I could see the castles better. Ahead of us, I could see the roads we would drive—they looked like veins or slashes across the rolling old mountain range, a thin black line between green pastures dotted here and there with strange, lean white cows with long horns. The sky over the mountains was heavy with clouds.

"The main castle is just up that ridge," Elora said from the backseat. I looked ahead and saw what I would have taken to be a pile of stones, gray and bare. If I tried hard, I could just make it out as having once been a human habitation.

We drove closer. "Do you want to go inside?" Elora asked from the backseat.

Patrizia spoke up. "Remember what happened before? How they said the next time they would shoot us if we went in the castle?"

"How would they know we're the same people?" Elora said, lighting a cigarette that quickly filled the car.

"I am not taking the risk," Patrizia said. "We can go to the lookout where it is permissible."

"You're getting soft, *bella*."

"I am not getting shot."

I opened my window as we drove down a hill. I lost sight of the castle and then the road turned and climbed a switchback up the hill, only wide enough for a single car. At the top, we were directly opposite the castle, and there was a place for cars to pull off the road to park. Patrizia turned off the car, and I helped Elora out of the backseat. There was a strong, cold wind blowing around us.

"It doesn't look exactly welcoming," I said.

"It was supposed to make people feel afraid or humiliated," Elora said.

"Humiliated?"

"*Andare a Canossa*," Patrizia said. "It is still said today. To go to Canossa—here—means to humble yourself or to be humiliated. It is the same thing."

I looked over at her, and wondered whether it was a language difference because to me the two were not the same at all.

Elora moved back into tour-guide mode. "The Pope was staying with Mathilda, and he had excommunicated one of the Henrys—the kings of France at the time—and Henry came in bare feet in the winter and begged the Pope to reinstate him in the church."

"He came here? In bare feet."

"In the snow," Patrizia said cheerfully.

"He made his way up to the castle and waited outside three days until the Pope agreed to see him. So 'to go to Canossa' means to do the same thing," Elora said.

I wrapped my sweater around me. It was cold enough up here in early April. I could not imagine three days in bare feet on this mountain in the winter.

"Maybe it is just a story," Patrizia said. "Who can know?"

I looked over at the castle, the ruins of the castle. Birds flew around it, and I could see the remains of windows.

"Did she live here alone?"

"She had two husbands and a daughter, but her daughter died soon after birth."

The bleakness of the castle now said jail rather than fortress.

It was late in the afternoon after we finished our tour of the castles of Mathilda, got back into the car and drove down off the ridge of mountains for our trip back. As we did, we passed farms like the ones we had seen on our way up. In the valley, the clouds cleared again to a blue sky and the air was warmer.

"Do we have time to stop to get cheese?" Patrizia asked. Without waiting for an answer, she pulled into a small dairy and we went inside with her. The young woman standing behind the counter offered me a sample of cheese, and I took it and realized that it was Parmesan.

"We're near Parma," Patrizia said, and she bought a wedge of the straw-colored cheese.

"I can't believe I'm in the place where Parmesan cheese actually comes from," I said.

"Balsamic vinegar, too," Elora said. "And Parma ham. It's good agricultural country here because of the soil."

I revised my thinking about the bleakness of Mathilda's castles.

We passed a variety of working dairies and cattle farms, and it reminded me of Waterloo County and the Mennonite farms in our area. Then we drove through a long grove of trees, and I saw a young woman standing among the trees, leaning against one. I wondered idly what she was doing and then fifty metres later there was another young woman, this one sitting on a metal chair, and then another in a plastic lawn chair. They all had jet black skin. I counted nine of them in the grove of trees.

"What are they doing here?" I asked. "Those women."

Patrizia and Elora both laughed. "*Puttane*," said Patrizia.

"*Puttane*?" I said.

"Whores," Elora said from the backseat, and my skin prickled with horror at the word and the reality.

Elora was still explaining. "They come here as migrants and they end up here on the trucking route."

The picture became clear: the women standing on the side of the road were like produce on display in a market. While we drove past them, others would stop and buy. And neither Elora nor Patrizia questioned this in the least but dismissed these women as less than human. I thought of the sex workers I'd met in the course of my work, the insults and injustices they suffered. I thought of how I'd tried to help.

The Italian countryside might look like home, but this was nothing like the Mennonite farm country in Waterloo Region.

The taste of Parmesan in my mouth suddenly was the taste of bile. I couldn't stop thinking about the women along the road. How did a trucker choose among them? How did they get onto this isolated road? Did they go into the bushes? Who had brought them there? Did anyone try to help them?

"It's awful," I said eventually. "Those poor women."

Patrizia shrugged. "Men," she said laconically.

I stared out the window, no longer taking in the countryside, wishing I could be at home. Patrizia turned the music up and drove while Elora snored in the backseat.

It was nearly dusk when we approached Florence at last, and the lights were fully on in the city when we came back over the mountains and into the valley split by the Arno River. I had wondered whether I would know the valley from the ones we traveled through as we drove back, but I did.

When we got stuck in traffic—I presumed the Florentine version of Sunday evening cottage country traffic—I fell asleep in the car, something I never did.

I woke up, disoriented, when Elora said, "We're here."

We were outside Patrizia's hair salon and their apartment, not the convent. "I should get back," I said, glancing at my watch. It was nearly nine. I had missed dinner, but I could make my curfew.

"Oh, come on, Cinderella," said Elora. "You won't turn into a pumpkin."

"A pumpkin?" Patrizia said, reaching for the bag of Parmesan cheese.

"You don't have that story here?" Elora said. "It's a Canadian thing?"

"I am making you a risotto," Patrizia said. "You will thank me."

Still half-asleep, I followed them into the building and up the stairs to the second floor where their apartment was.

"*Mamma mia*," Elora said, kicking off her shoes at the door. "I need a shower."

Patrizia took off her shoes and then removed her bra from under her sweater, sighing as she did so.

"Can I help with supper?" I asked. It had been weeks since I had cooked.

"I will start the onions for the risotto," she said. "You just sit."

I went into their living room and sat down on the couch.

Patrizia came out in a minute. She held a box of cigarettes toward me. "I will have a cigarette while the onions sweat. You?"

I shook my head.

She turned on the television and opened the door to the balcony. The smell of the cigarette mingled with the scent of onions and butter. That and the cacophony on the television, and the fact that I wanted to go back to the convent made me feel that this place was no homier than the ruined castles we'd visited that afternoon.

I joined Patrizia in the kitchen as she cooked, and I sat on a bright red stool. She was older than Elora and me, and she looked even older in the harsh florescent light.

"Do you have children?" I asked her.

She smiled. "*Sì.* I have a son."

She poured wine and stock into the rice, as she told me stories about her son, who lived in America, as she called it. "They have the all-day breakfast," she said. "That is the only advantage of America I can see." She FaceTimed with him, and with his children, who called her *nonna*.

"And his father?"

She turned the risotto hard with her spoon. "My useless husband? He's gone now."

Elora came into the room, her hair in a towel, her face strangely free of the heavy makeup she always wore. She was dressed in a salmon-colored robe, cinched at her waist, and it was the first color I had seen her wear since I had met her in Italy. It was her face that struck me, heavy, doughy, almost bloated. I looked for the face I had known briefly all those years ago, and I wondered whether I had imagined that face over the years as more delicate and fairy-like than it had been.

Patrizia grated the Parmesan and handed me a piece that broke off, but I couldn't eat it after that afternoon. I crumbled it into the pile with the rest. She chopped pieces of ham and stirred them into the risotto and then added a pile of grated cheese that took two hands.

"Salad, *cara*?" she said to Elora.

"I can make it," I said.

She pointed to the refrigerator. "*Roquette*," she said. "It is in the bottom drawer."

The refrigerator was filled with bottled water, tubs of olives and cheese, and, unexpectedly, dozens of pill bottles. I wondered whether there was anything in this refrigerator that was the same as in my fridge at home.

"This?" I said, pulling out a bag of dark green leaves.

She glanced over. "*Si.*" I rinsed the greens over a sink filled with dirty wine glasses and a ceramic bowl filled with cigarette ashes and olive pits.

Patrizia pulled six bowls down from a cupboard and began spooning risotto into three of them. She motioned to me to distribute the *roquette* between the other three. She grated more Parmesan on the top of the risotto and onto the *roquette*, and then drizzled olive oil and thick dark vinegar over the salad and finished with pepper over everything.

"*Vino?*" she asked.

"Always," Elora said, and she took three enormous glasses from the sink and poured soap into each before rinsing them out and then filling them with a dark purple wine. I would call a taxi to get home after supper, I decided, taking a glass of wine from Elora.

Patrizia brought a third chair from the living room to join the two chairs at the counter in the kitchen. She lit a candle and turned off the lights.

"Now it is romantic," she said.

It was not romantic but it was delicious. As I ate and drank, I realized I had been anxious and tired because of hunger. Soon I relaxed and enjoyed the simple meal.

When we finished, I looked at my watch and it was five to eleven. "I *am* Cinderella now," I said. "They lock the gates for the night at eleven."

"So stay here," Elora said. "I have to go into the city in the morning for a tour. We can take the bus together."

Honey popped into my mind. I found my phone and quickly texted her to tell her where I was.

She texted back almost instantly, in caps. *I WAS WORRIED. I THOUGHT YOU WOULD BE BACK BEFORE SUPPER.*

So did I, I wrote back. *I'm really sorry. But I'm okay. I'm staying with friends.*

The three of us sat on the couch and listened to the noises outside, which were different from the noises at the convent. There were fewer bells here, and more sirens. Elora and Patrizia watched television, and then Elora found me a set of sheets and a blanket, and she covered one of the pillows on the couch.

I washed my face and rinsed my mouth in the bathroom that was covered with pill bottles and lotions and shampoo bottles. I had not brought anything with me, so I did what

Patrizia had done earlier, simply taking off my bra so that I could sleep more comfortably in my clothes.

When I came out again, Elora was bent over beside the couch. "I'm just checking to make sure the heating is off," she said when she saw me.

"Thanks," I said. I yawned. "Good night."

I covered myself with the sheets and pulled the blanket up to my neck. I missed the Virgin Mary on the wall watching me, but I soon fell asleep.

I rolled over a little while later and saw Elora nearby.

"Hey," I said, half-awake.

"*Shhh,*" she said. "I'm putting your gas money back in your purse. Don't tell Patrizia. Today was my treat for you."

"I don't mind," I said. "I was glad you took me to the castles."

"Sometimes I call her Mathilda. I think she likes it."

I fell back asleep.

34

In my work, I often met people at the moment their life diverged from where they thought it was going, the moment two pathways opened up—neither one desirable—when they had to figure out what to do. When I met Naomi, that path had splintered so long ago that going back wasn't an option, that it was hard for her to even remember what she had hoped for her life.

Naomi was about my age. She was tall and thin with long dark hair. She had two kids. And she was a sex worker.

I met her when she came into our office one day in a panic. "They're trying to take my babies away. Can you help me?"

There was enough overlap with our organization's mission to say yes, but I wouldn't have turned her away anyhow. She explained that she had to go to court that morning and that her son was in school but her usual childcare had fallen through at the last moment. Naomi was going to court because someone had called the Children's Aid Society on her, saying that a ten-year-old boy was too old to share a room with his sister and mother, that Naomi was a hooker and a druggie, and she shouldn't have custody of the children.

She asked whether she could leave her daughter with us while she went to court that morning to try to keep custody of her children. We gave the little girl, Ava, a set of highlighter markers and some flipchart paper and she drew small pictures in the corner of the large paper. Our receptionist gave her a doughnut and she ate it in amazement, her first doughnut in her three years of life. Ava was polite, and her hair was neatly combed and separated into two high ponytails. She wore two tiny studs in her ears.

Naomi came back an hour later to say that the case had been postponed until she could be assigned a lawyer. She thanked us for looking after her daughter, saying she had had nowhere else to turn.

I thought about Naomi all that week. I thought about her when I went home to my nice Beechwood house, how much more in common I might have with the person who called the Children's Aid Society than with Naomi.

But it had not been that person who had come into my office. It had been a mother who adored her children, who sacrificed for her children, who took good care of her children. She challenged the simplistic categories I had unconsciously adopted about what a good mother was.

I wondered whether she would bring her daughter back when she went to court the following week, but she didn't. It worried me: she had had no other option other than to leave her daughter with strangers. What had become of her?

A month or so later I saw Naomi in the grocery store near the center, and she was buying lentils. I wasn't sure whether I should speak to her but I felt like I had to.

"I don't know if you remember me," I said.

She looked up, the fear that instantly flooded her expression quickly replaced by recognition. "You're one of the ladies from that center, right?" she said.

"That's right," I said. "I've been wondering how you are, how your kids are."

She took in a quick breath and shook her head. "They put my kids in foster care. Until I can get a legal job and prove I've been drug-free for six months."

"I'm sorry," I said, and I was. Not for the first time, I wished somehow I could make everything better, for Naomi, for Ava, for her son.

"They're my motivation," she said, tears filling her eyes. "But I don't know whether I can do it without them."

They couldn't just take someone's kids, could they? I thought. Or maybe they only wouldn't if you lived in a nice house and had a nice job.

I knew an executive director whose program included an addictions program for women, and I offered to take Naomi to see it, but she said she already was part of a different program. I wasn't sure what to do then. Just go back to my privileged life? I wasn't sure if I should hug her or buy her groceries or what. The questions were too big for me.

"I believe in you," I said, finally.

For months I prayed for Naomi and her kids every night. I thought about her and spoke up when I heard anyone speak disdainfully about a sex worker. And I nearly threw up while driving later that winter when I saw Naomi panhandling on a city corner. The light turned green, someone behind me honked their horn, and I drove off before I could stop to ask whether she had regained her kids or whether she had lost even more than she had before.

35

I KNEW IT WOULD STILL BE WINTER AT HOME, or at the very least it would be gray with lumps of snow in the shadows and at the edge of driveways. It would be another month until the bulbs I planted poked their heads above ground.

Here, spring had begun with the mimosas everywhere in the streets on International Women's Day, the scentless yellow balls. This was followed by the appearance of cheerful primulas in shop window boxes. On the first of April, Niccolò had opened the doors of the *limonaia* to prepare the potted lemon trees to be carted outside for the summer, and the smell that came from the greenhouse was one I associated with Florida, with its waxy, white citrus blossoms. I was still waiting for the magnificence that I was told would be the *glicine*.

Magnifico was the word they used when they said, "You should see the *glicine* when it's in bloom." It was the same word that was used of Lorenzo de' Medici. The plant might be a thousand years old, might be espaliered against an ancient stone wall once owned by a friend of Galileo, but it had not looked magnificent to me. Still, I kept an eye on it and its buds began to open, some forming into leaves and others that resembled purple raspberries with each small segment beginning to open into flowers.

Then one day I walked outside into the gardens and stepped straight into a profusion of tiny violets that had sprung up seemingly overnight through the grass along the slopes and among the olive trees behind the villa. They were everywhere and I wondered how they could have come up so suddenly. I wanted to call Russ to ask him whether somehow there was a carpet of tiny blue scilla stars in bloom at our house.

The air was scented with the quiet candy-sweetness of the violets, and the smell came to me on soft breezes. I walked in the garden down the pathways as though I were a princess in a fairy tale or Eve in the garden.

It made me think: Eve in the garden without Cain and Abel, even without Adam. It had never just been Eve—but Eve had existed before the pain of childbirth, before *the desire for your husband and he will rule over you*, before sin.

I thought of Mary. Who had been enough without a human partner. Who had been blessed among women. Who had been the perfect mother. Mary in the garden when the power of the Most High overshadowed her.

Let it be unto me, Mary had said, simply accepting. Had she had her own experience of being midway on life's journey? The *Pietà* I had seen given me pause: could you hold the broken body of your child and still say, *let it be unto me*?

I thought of the women who could never say those words, the women I'd seen on the side of the road—the women in the grove near Parma and Naomi in my own town—whose bodies had been broken by power overshadowing them, who were cast out of the garden by sin that wasn't their own. How could anyone expect them to say, *let it be unto me*? I saw them in my mind's eye, both alive and dead simultaneously. *Darling*, I thought, picturing Naomi, *if only we had a bomb.*

All these questions were vital ones, but they were too big for me, too much, wrong even on a day when violets appeared in lavish profusion. I did not have to accept everything in the world on this day, but I had been given the choice to accept the gift of violets blossoming all around me.

And I did.

I sank into the grass. All the novels and films about Italy, all the stories about midlife crisis would have me have an affair, maybe with one of the monks, would have me rediscover passion in this way. But this was not that story, any more than Eve's story was mine or Naomi's. This was my life, my real life, and in this life I was wooed in the garden, tenderly, passionately, simply with the gift of violets. They had not been planted for me, but I dared to believe in the possibility that they bloomed for me.

36

THE WORLD HAD OPENED UP FOR ME ONE SUMMER, the summer before my last year of high school. That summer I worked as a mother's helper for my art teacher so she could paint in her flower garden without her twin toddlers getting underfoot.

What I remember of that summer is like a collage. My teacher playing Leonard Cohen music when all my friends were listening to Top 40 songs. My teacher's house, with its masses of white filmy curtains in every window so that the entire house gave me the sensation of being in a cloud. Her wild garden with raspberries and cherry tomato plants mixed among flowers, and toddlers emerging from pathways between tall grasses. Her paintings, enormous canvases bigger than she was, with bold colors and paint so thickly applied they were almost sculptural. Her husband coming home early one day, while I was still there, kissing her on the side of her neck as she painted.

I used my babysitting money to buy white curtains to turn my room into as much of a cloud as I could.

Every day, I biked to her house. On my way, I began to notice a building I'd never paid attention to before, a tall old church. It was a Catholic church, the kind of church my mother had warned me against. The Catholic Church, according to my mother, would teach you false doctrine and heresy and would convert you and lead you astray. I felt both drawn to it and afraid of it, but I decided that I would go in before the summer was over, that I was old enough now to see for myself.

It was the second to last day of the summer when I got up my nerve, only to discover that the door was locked between services. I had one day left before school started and when I saw there was a mass at nine the next morning and my teacher didn't need me until ten, I decided I would go to that service.

The church was dark and heavy inside, although warm in the heat of the day. There were only slivers of windows. I deliberately arrived three minutes late so that I could slip inside after the service had begun, but it was shadowy enough that I didn't have to worry about that. I sat in the back pew near the door.

The church smelled of furniture polish and beeswax and something I would later discover was incense. I felt extraordinarily grown up, with a sense that the world was opening like a flower, that everything good was ahead. High up at the front of the church, illuminated, was a figure on a cross.

In twenty minutes, the service was done and I was back on my bicycle. I was early to work and I found my art teacher in the garden with a toddler in each arm, feeding them. She looked up and wrinkled her nose at me.

"It'll be hard to go back to school, won't it?"

It was, and yet somehow I took a sense of possibility and passion from that summer as I went forward, a sense that smelled of flowers and incense and beeswax and oil paintings and milky toddlers and raspberries, a darkened church, a cloud-filled room, a kiss on the neck, and the deep voice of Leonard Cohen purring beneath it all.

37

"LIZ? WHAT HAPPENED?" MY RINGING PHONE HAD wakened me. It was Russ.

"What's wrong?" I said. "What do you mean? Nothing's happened."

It was six-thirty in the morning, and it was getting light out because we had shifted to Daylight Savings Time.

"The gynecologist procedure," he said, sounding shaken. "They sent the report of the claim. I've been waiting to call you when it was morning your time."

I rubbed my eyes. "What report? I don't know what you're talking about."

"Liz," he said, "I know you want your space but you need to tell me if you have surgery."

I did a double take. "Surgery? I'm not having surgery. I didn't have surgery. I would have told you if I had surgery. I promise you'd be the first to know, but I didn't have any surgery. What are you talking about?"

I heard him exhale, could picture him running his hands through his hair.

"You got a report?" I asked.

"It says gynecological procedure at a hospital in Florence on the tenth. Tuesday the tenth."

"I swear to you I'd remember if I went to the hospital. I was pruning trees that day. It's got to be a mistake."

"But, it's Florence. That doesn't seem random. Is there any chance you lost your health insurance card?"

"I don't think so, but I'll check," I said, getting out of bed and finding my purse. I opened it to the pocket where I had put my travel health insurance card. My heart sank: it wasn't there.

I began rifling through all the pockets and slots in the leather. Finally I looked in the zippered pouch on the outside of my purse, and there it was along with a roll of euro bills.

I went back to Russ. I had begun to shake. "I've got it," I said. "I'll make some calls and sort this out. But I'm okay."

He let out a deep breath. "I love you, you know," he said.

"I know," I said. I had to get off the phone. "OK, I'll call you soon."

I knew what had happened the moment I found the card with the euros. I thought back to the night I slept over at Elora's apartment, how I woke in the night to find her reaching into my bag. She had explained it as putting back the gas money I had given her for the road trip, and I had believed her. But she had lied to me and was putting back my stolen health insurance card.

We were moving the lemon trees out of the *limonaia* that morning.

"You're quiet," Honey said.

It was like when I was in labor. I went very deep inside myself. I wasn't one of the women who screamed in pain, was not aware of anything other than the contractions that took over my body and sent me deep within to ride out the storm. I went far down inside myself now too.

We unwrapped the burlap that surrounded the lemon trees, keeping them warm for the winter. The small fibers were prickly and painful on my hands, and it was one irritation too many. I folded the burlap but I just wanted to ball it up and throw it away.

How had I been so naïve? I would make the worst customs agent, unable to tell counterfeit from real. What had made me trust Elora for a moment? When we were children, I had admired her but we had never been friends. When I met her again, it wasn't like we had something to reminisce about. For a brief moment as Honey and I pushed the extraordinarily heavy clay pots across the floor of the *limonaia*, I wondered whether this even truly was Elora Lowe. It had been hard for me to see the features of the child she'd been in the woman she was. I ran over the big toe of my left foot with the pot.

"Fuck!" I said.

"Are you okay?" Honey asked.

My toe throbbed. "I'm fine."

"I mean, I didn't know you even knew that word."

All morning I moved impossibly heavy objects out into the sunshine while inside my head I ran the moves of the chess game I had played. I had been careful about pickpockets. I had thrown out my whistle, believing that people were essentially good, that God would protect me. Where had it gotten me, idealism, this unwillingness to look at what was *real*?

When we broke for lunch, I checked the website for *La Dolce Vita* to see if Elora was hosting a tour that day: there was an afternoon Uffizi tour meeting at one. I told Honey I needed to go into town, that I had an errand to run. I would try to be back by the time we started again for the afternoon, but if I wasn't . . . I left the sentence dangling. What were they going to do if I didn't show up? I no longer idealized them or felt like I needed to meet their approval. It seemed like a bad idea to idealize anyone.

As I ran down the hill to catch the bus, I could feel fury building inside me. If someone pushed me on the bus, or pinched me, God help them. I saw the bitter woman with the cigarette in the piazza, still wrapped in woolens despite the warmth of the day, her back turned away from the art and natural beauty of the city. I wondered whether a cigarette could keep someone from screaming.

I was anything but a tourist in the heat of the day, my eyes blinkered to the beauty, irritated by the slow-moving oohing and ahhing tourists. I dashed through the streets and found myself in the shade of the Colonnade, the courtyard of the Uffizi, surrounded by the witnesses of the statues of the leading citizens of historical Florence. I saw Dante. A number of tourist groups were beginning to form. I looked for Elora's peacock feather and found her stationed beneath the statue of Lorenzo, dressed fully in black despite the heat of the day.

"How dare you?" I said as soon as I reached her. "How dare you do this to me?"

Elora looked at me as though no one had ever questioned her before.

"You stole my health insurance."

She took me by the arm, smiling a firmly fixed smile at the couple coming toward her, and led me out into the piazza where she took her tours for hot chocolate, the piazza where the Italian had been stabbed to death in *A Room With A View.*

"I borrowed it, yes."

"You *stole* it. What if I had needed it?"

To my astonishment, she shrugged. "I stole from the insurance system, not from you. It was back before you even knew it was gone. If you'd needed it, you could have reported it stolen and had it replaced."

I remembered the girl who channeled Elvis in a séance, who knew what *conceived* meant when she was eight years old, who plucked a feather from a peacock when she won a poker game, who inexplicably befriended me and took me under her wing.

It was less inexplicable now.

"It's all a lie, isn't it? You wanted to take the easy way out and to get something for nothing and you pretended to be my friend so that you could steal my insurance. How dare you? I trusted you and you took my identity while I slept."

"Actually I put it back while you slept. Keep your voice down, would you."

"You don't get it. Do you think it's a small thing to take someone's identity? And it's not just about identity—it's about trust. If you needed help, you could have asked. You assumed what I would say and you had no fucking idea." My anger was building. "I fucking trusted you and this is how you fucking repay me? You could have trusted me. If you needed help you could have asked me. You could have fucking trusted that I would do what I could to help."

I was heaving with sobs by this point. I had never in my life even been tempted to hit anyone and now my hands were forming themselves into fists as if they knew that finally violence was called for.

"What are you talking about, you crazy person?" Elora said, smiling nervously.

"Just because you fucking felt like it. Well, fuck you!"

Now she looked at me, her eyes hard. "Fuck *you*. I needed surgery badly."

"I'm not a fool, Elora."

"I'm not lying to you. Here—" She dug around in her bag and came out with a piece of paper and shoved it into my hands. It was written in Italian. I threw it back at her.

"Put it in Google Translate," she said and did so herself. She handed her phone to me. "Don't throw it."

The words—*rimozione della cisti ovarica*—were translated: ovarian cyst removal. I looked at her.

"I don't have time for this," she said, taking her phone back. "I have a tour starting."

"Make time," I said between clenched teeth.

"Fine. It's been killing me every other month—every time I ovulate on the left side. I mean really killing me. I don't schedule tours on the week of every other period because I faint from the pain and I have to stay in bed. Only now, probably I will be okay again. But, fuck, Liz, what the fuck is this about?"

I took a deep breath. I knew what this was about. I knew exactly what the fuck this was about.

38

"WHY DIDN'T THEY COME TO ME?" I ASKED RUSS ONE DAY while we were wrapping Christmas presents. We had been over the territory so many times by that point that Russ didn't even need references as to who and for what.

"They knew what you would say," he said.

"How would they know what I would say?" I asked.

"Honey, what else would you say? It would be like asking the butcher whether you should go vegetarian."

I drew in a quick breath. "That's cruel."

"It's what Jackson said when I suggested he talk to you."

My pulse throbbed in my ears. "What do you mean?"

"Never mind," Russ said. "What's done is done."

"You knew?" I said. "Beforehand?"

Russ shrugged.

I ran to the bathroom and threw up. He had known even before the abortion.

"Are you okay? You don't have to make such a big deal out of this, Liz," Russ said through the locked door of the bathroom.

I sat on the floor and shook, my throat raw from vomiting as it had not been since I was pregnant with Timothy. Russ had known when the baby was still alive. He had known and he hadn't told me. And Jackson had likened it—likened me—to a butcher advising someone about their food choices. I threw up again, and I lay on the bathroom floor until I fell asleep.

When I woke it was the middle of the night. Russ had left my bedside lamp on low—for when I stopped making a big deal out of things, I supposed. I stood in the doorway of our bedroom and I had no idea what to do, who to talk to, where to go.

39

I KNEW IT WAS HONEY LEAVING TO GO TO THE AIRPORT when I awoke to the sound of a car door closing outside on Sunday morning. I thought of the conversation we'd had on the orange couch, feet to feet, the night before when I told her the whole story about Elora and the health insurance.

"I'm such a fool," I'd said.

Honey propped herself up on her elbows. "My folks have people stay with us all the time and each one shows up with the nicest hostess gift, but it only takes a few days to know what they're really like. I've lived with you for weeks. You're not a fool. Even with this chick."

"I liked living with you too," I said. "I'm going to miss you."

"All these sights and sounds and smells will be yours to enjoy, Wilbur—this lovely world, these precious days . . .," Honey said.

I felt my heart swell: she was quoting the end of *Charlotte's Web*. "I hope it goes okay with your mom," I said, welling up with tears.

"If not, I'll come to Canada and stay with you."

"It's a deal," I said, and I hugged her before we went to bed.

I knew I would miss Honey during my last weeks in Italy and at the same time part of me was glad to be alone. I forced myself to get up and go down the hill to the English Church, and then I found I could not make myself go inside. I walked back to the convent, striding so hard my calves began to hurt, wishing I still had my whistle, wishing I could just blow it until I had no breath left. I was sweating by the time I got back and yet I couldn't sit still.

I went down the hill to the circle of cypress trees where Honey and I had sunbathed. I remembered her story about Hitler and Mussolini and the wish for a bomb, for destruction that would undo all past and future destruction.

"Midway on life's journey I found myself alone in a dark wood," I said aloud, and then I felt like I was being dramatic and foolish—like I was making *such* a big deal out of this—and instead I wandered into the olive grove, which was still filled with tiny violets and trees that were pruned and ready to grow.

Niccolò had told us that one of the reasons pruning was done in the winter was that while olive trees never fully shed their leaves, in winter we could see better what was going on, to figure out where branches had crossed, to understand which branches were the main ones, which blocked the light and the growth of the trees.

It was precisely how I felt about examining my marriage, that I needed to look at it hard before cutting into it. My father had always said when it came to carpentry: measure twice, cut once. The same was true for pruning olive trees and even more so for evaluating marriage.

I walked through the grove toward the tree that had been hit by lightning. It felt like my marriage, black and damaged. And yet, Niccolò had surprised me by keeping that tree when he had entirely taken down the other trees. "Sometimes," he said, "sometimes a healthy shoot grows out of such a tree, growing from its roots. We will know by the autumn."

It was very much like what I had been attempting to do by coming to Italy, but I was afraid of going back home. The olive trees were resilient and needed large egregious wounds in order to bear fruit, but some of them would not survive damage from lightning strikes and ice storms. I was afraid to face Russ and my family again. What would I go back to? What if there was no life left in my marriage or my family, or even in myself? Where would I go if I could not go back?

I looked hard at the tree for any signs of life. I could see nothing but char.

I remembered the time Russ had once gone out for lunch to a Vietnamese restaurant with colleagues. He had ordered a bowl of soup and it came with a little addition that hadn't been mentioned on the menu: an entire baby squid, looking up at him.

This had become our shorthand way of talking about situations where someone wanted to avoid something unpleasant and obvious: "I think there's a squid in the soup here," Russ or I would say, whether it was the boys pretending they hadn't broken a window or were trying to explain away a C- on a report card.

It was what I said to myself as I sat in the grass in front of the lightning-struck olive tree. *There's a squid in the soup.*

My rage at Elora stealing my card made me certain that what had broken my heart hadn't been the baby. As sad as that had been—super-sad, as Honey had said—my grief was that they assumed I would make things worse, that none of them trusted that I could offer anything good to a sad situation. They kept the truth from me. And it was that Russ hadn't trusted me.

Was I a fool?

40

Midway on life's journey I found myself alone in a dark wood where the right way was lost. I said those words to myself the day I left Joanna and the retreat center, the day I found out about the abortion and didn't know where to go. I said those words to myself the night I found out that Russ had known about the abortion before it happened, that he had not trusted me with the truth.

I talked with Russ the day after I barricaded myself in the bathroom for the night.

"I didn't know what to do," Russ said.

"Did you consider even for a moment that I might know what to do?" I felt rage rising within me.

Russ looked at me patiently. "If they had been uncertain, I'm sure they would have come to you." I could tell he was trying to be reassuring, consoling, reasonable.

"Let me tell you something I know, something that you wouldn't know," I said. "When people come to you in a situation like this, only occasionally do they present as undecided. It's hard enough just to give the facts. They usually say, 'so I've decided to keep the baby,' or 'we've decided to terminate the pregnancy.' We call that an opening statement. We always tell our volunteers to hold those statements loosely. To respect them and at the same time to understand that they are provisional statements, regardless of how strongly they say them."

I could feel myself slipping into executive director mode, and it felt purposeful: I wanted Russ to see what he clearly hadn't seen in the spring, that I was capable and that there were best practices, a distinct methodology to this, better and worse ways of dealing with this kind of situation.

I could see Russ replaying his moves in his head, but I still wasn't sure he saw the tightrope I walked every day.

"What do you think we *do* at the pregnancy center?" I asked, my voice rising. "Do you think we just tell our clients what they have to do? That we fall to pieces if someone has an abortion? That we shame them or tie them up so they can't go ahead with it—?"

Even though I had wanted the executive director job ten years ago, I had made it clear even at my first interview that I would not be open to showing gory pictures of disembodied fetuses to scare women into keeping their babies. I had fired more than one volunteer who had used coercive, bullying tactics on vulnerable clients. "We are pro-life," I said countless times. "We want to help everyone have a healthy life. Not just babies."

I thought suddenly of our bookkeeper, how she had come to me to tell me she'd had an abortion, how she couldn't afford a van and one more kid would mean they didn't fit in their car, how she was turning forty and was worried what she would possibly do if the baby was disabled. In a perfect world, every pregnancy would happen at the right time to people who were overjoyed about having a baby, and no one would ever face the pain or the choices women like Jenn agonized over. I had told her what I always told our volunteers, that the sooner you recognize how painful and hard and wrenching this is for our clients, the better you'll be at your job, supporting our clients as they make their choices, but that we couldn't make situations all better.

"Stop," Russ said, his face showing—what? Realization? Defeat? "I should have told you. I should have told them to tell you. And I didn't."

"Why didn't you?"

I knew going into this work that some people would assume I was one of those who shamed women and who saw the world in clear-cut terms of right and wrong, black and white. I also knew that for most people this was a binary issue: you were either for us or against us. What had surprised me—even if maybe I should have known better—were the people on both sides of that divide who presumed my nuanced stance was a deceptive cover for the other side, that at some level, I was lying to them. A sad reality of my work. But I had always believed that those who knew me would *know* me.

"I don't know," Russ said, quietly. That was the last we spoke of it as I prepared to leave for Italy.

41

The weather was the exact opposite of pathetic fallacy. Everything was in bloom and it was sunny and warm—piazza weather—and there I was, like the old Italian woman from the *tabacchi*, smoking as though her cigarette was a lifeline when really it accelerated death, scratching at her lottery ticket as though she knew from the outset she would not win. What would she do if she won the lottery, I wondered. What did she dream of, hope for? She never made eye contact with me, or with anyone.

That woman in her black woolens became an image of warning to me, a figure of grief turned to bitterness. Her black clothes and smoking didn't distinguish her particularly—there were countless people like her across Italy—but she presented such a different picture from the men who sat in piazzas and smoked with an air of wellbeing and satisfaction or the nuns in their powder-blue habits, visiting the Pinocchio Park, singing their masses, pressing their olives, cooking meals for guests.

The next time I saw her, though, I thought of the *Pietà* in the museum, the grief of Mary bearing her own burden.

I sat on my bed and talked with the picture of Mary on the wall, "How?" I asked her. "How did you not turn bitter? How did you not let your sorrows poison you?" Of course, my question was really: how can I bear this pain? How do I not turn as bitter as the *tabacchi* woman?

For all I knew the *tabacchi* woman was bitter because she had never won the lottery, but even that, at some level, meant she had a hole she was trying to fill. I had told Honey at the Pinocchio Park that the dreadful hole in the center of my life wasn't simple, and I had meant that it was about far more than the abortion. It was about Russ and the boys and my work and my anger at being left out of the conversation. That was why I had escaped to Italy. But I saw in myself now that it was even more complicated, that all that sorrow and anger could turn to bitterness I couldn't run away from.

I thought of the *tabacchi* woman as Niccolò directed the planting of new olive trees in the area struck by the storm. He brought other brothers from another monastery to help. It turned out they were monks from San Miniato—some of those I'd heard sing Vespers—and I strangely felt as though I was in the presence of celebrity. The monks carried the baby olive trees, five feet tall, while I dug holes for the trees where Niccolò indicated. He made me dig deeper than I thought we would need to, and then had me bring buckets of water to fill the holes, soaking the ground, before the trees were placed.

With each hole I dug I thought again of the bitter old woman and the gaping wounds in my own life. What did you do when a storm came and destroyed ancient trees you had nurtured and tended? How could I read this other than as metaphor?

As we were finishing planting the new olive trees, a new pair of volunteers arrived, two young women from Japan who spoke fluent Italian but almost no English. Salvia and *Madre* Maria-Catarina came to put them in *Jesus, Bloody Jesus* and in the *Finger Pointing* room. I wondered whether it was my responsibility to pass on the traditions of the volunteers, to initiate foot-rubbing, to tell them that the apartment was called Lemonland, to tell them about the eleven o'clock curfew, to let them know that they shouldn't talk to the nuns about personal matters. I decided it wasn't my responsibility, that I was off the job as mother hen.

They came out to the olive groves as we planted the trees, taking pictures of us and themselves with the olive trees. One of them picked up a withered olive from the ground and put it in her mouth before I could warn her about its unpleasant bitterness. She spat it out immediately.

It made me think of when the boys wanted to help in the kitchen when they were small, how they had made what they called concoctions to feed one another. At first, before I realized their aims, I didn't know that they were trying to see who could make the vilest-tasting concoctions. We had a conversation about not wasting food, about not making your brothers sick, about the kindness of making food for other people. I began to teach them to cook vegetables instead. One night Timothy made Brussels sprouts and they were as harsh as a concoction or a raw olive. We added in a spoonful of sugar and a pinch of salt and caramelized the sprouts in a pan, redeeming the taste.

What could take this bitterness away from me?

I thought of a painting I had seen in one of the museums, of a mother who lost her sons and then changed her name from one that meant pleasant to one that meant bitter. I turned that word—*bitter*—over in my mouth all day as I planted trees. For years, my life had been pleasant. And now? The concoction of my life had taken on an acrid taste.

42

There was one thing that kept coming to mind, although it was so slight that I wondered whether I had dreamed it. It was so small that I could never know.

It had been a single text last spring.

After I found out about the abortion, I scrolled back through the messages on my phone until my thumb ached, searching to see if there had been any clues, any signs. I found a single text from Jackson that I had never answered, had never paid attention to. It said, *Mom, you there?* I had ignored it because I saw the second text first, three hours later, the text that read *NM*: never mind.

It haunted me all winter. What had happened during those three hours?

The first time Timothy came home from university, I suggested he wear a coat, and he tartly reminded me that he had survived seven weeks of living on his own. It was a fair comment, a reminder that he was successfully independent and able to look after himself. But as I looked in my calendar for what I had been doing the day of Jackson's text last spring, I discovered it was the day I'd been in training for our new data management system, and we'd been asked to turn off our phones. That seemed fair, too. But it was so maddeningly wrong that one of my few windows of being inaccessible could have been my one small opportunity to be included in this conversation.

The frustration faded but the guilt did not. I tried to remind myself that it equally could have been a question about whether a best-before label on yogurt meant it was toxic after that date. It could have been.

Recalling this small unanswered message also allowed me to dare hope that there was a space in my son that respected my opinion or that maybe Jackson did not see me only as a butcher but as a mom he wanted to comfort from. It could have been.

43

One day at lunch, an envelope was waiting for me on my table. Kaito and Sora, the new volunteers, sat down across from me. Our conversation consisted mostly of sign language and smiling, and my feeble attempts at speaking Italian with them. I was decent at communicating numbers, my nationality and giving directions, but much more than that was beyond me. But I had no language, not even in English, when I picked up the letter and saw it was from Jackson.

We had begun weeding the gardens that morning in advance of planting annuals. We had more weeding to do that afternoon after our rest period, but now I felt a compulsion to be in the belly of San Miniato, in the crypt, in my church away from home, in a place where there was predictability and faithfulness and goodness and devotion and order.

"*Scusi*," I said to Kaito and Sora. I picked up my letter and left without eating.

As I stepped up the dozens of wide stone stairs that led to San Miniato, I thought of the day Joanna accidentally told me about the baby, how I had stepped over the stones of the labyrinth, the lines that would have held me safely in their pathways. I had crossed other lines, with Elora, with my language—I had said *the F word,* as my boys called it, at least in front of me—more times than I had in my whole life. And yet, if I was honest, it had been my prayer for months. It was the word I said over and over again under my breath this last year. I'd read that people who swear are healthier and better adjusted people than those who don't swear, but I had never before felt a need to swear, until this last year. In my mother's eyes it was the worst of the swear words because it profaned something private and holy, she had explained when a friend of mine once said it in her hearing.

As I climbed higher toward the church, surrounded by more tourists than I'd seen before at San Miniato, I realized it was perhaps the right word, not simply because of the degree of my frustration—*honestly, my* fucking *anger*—but also because it was a word that had to do precisely with where I had been wounded: in my womb, in my deepest core, my most tender and private and lifegiving place. There had been death upon death in that place. *Fuck* was my prayer and I wasn't entirely sure that God would correct me for it.

I thought of a story I'd read in my guidebook about the ascent to San Miniato. There once was a man—a count—whose brother had been killed. The count was climbing the hill I was now on when he came upon his brother's murderer and raised a hand to kill the murderer in revenge. When the murderer pleaded for his life, saying it was Good Friday, the count released him and went on his way up the hill to the church of San Miniato where, the story went, the figure on the cross bowed his head to the count in recognition of his generous and merciful sparing of the murderer. The guidebook said that the count begged pardon of his own sins, cut off his hair and entered the monastery as a monk, although he had previously been a worldly man.

I felt sweat bead on the naked nape of my neck. I had done it backwards: I had come to church without forgiveness—what would I do if, ascending, I met Russ? Or if I were faced with Caitlin and Jackson? Could I stop holding this against them? What did Jackson's letter say? What would he accuse me of? I could not read it yet.

I did not go down into the crypt where the Vespers were sung. Instead I walked all over the vast church looking in nooks and crannies for the crucifix from the story. I wanted . . . something. A head to bow at me? I felt sillier than I did about talking with the portrait of Mary on my wall but I needed to see the crucifix.

Finally I paid two euros for a set of headphones that gave me a stilted English tour of the church. Eventually it directed me to the chapel that had been built to house the crucifix that bowed its head at the count. When I arrived at the chapel, a small sign told me the crucifix had been moved to another church. It felt like a terrible scavenger hunt—and to what end? I was looking for God, was searching for something as serious or perhaps as superstitious as the relic of a saint's mummified finger in a museum.

Sitting down, I leaned back in a pew, weary. I closed my eyes, conscious of the letter in my pocket. I still couldn't open it. It was good to sit in the quiet, to hear the hush of voices and the soft tapping of feet around me. I wanted to pray but I didn't know what I should pray for, and my F-word prayer didn't seem to express what I wanted to say this time. I thought of the astronomer at the convent that first morning, his experiment about the cat in the box. Right now, with the unopened letter, I was both mother and not-mother. I dreaded the possibility of opening the letter to find myself blamed, indicted, fired.

I sat in the pew until my muscles began to ache from sitting on the hard wood. I could not stay in this place forever. With a sigh, I opened my eyes and saw a figure of Jesus giving the peace sign. He was the central figure in a mosaic just above me. I had glanced at the mosaic during my audio tour of the church, but I hadn't really looked at it and I hadn't realized it was in front of me when I sat down. On one side of Jesus, the audio tour had said, was Saint Minias, the first martyr of Florence, for whom the church had been named. Saint Minias had been thoroughly persecuted for his faith—he had been stoned, had his head chopped off, and was fed to the lions—

but he lived long enough afterwards, legend said, to carry his own severed head up the hill to what was now his final resting place in the crypt beneath me. In the mosaic, he was presenting a crown to Jesus. On the other side of Jesus was his mother, Mary, standing with her hands open.

What was it to be a mother? What was it to suffer for your love? What was it to be right? What did it mean to show mercy? What would I say if Jackson accused me?

I thought of something I'd heard years before at an earlier church retreat I'd been on with Joanna. The retreat leader speaking on a psalm that said, *Let all that is within me bless His holy name*, encouraged us to simply to offer whatever we had to God. I thought about what I had within me: I had sorrow. I had weariness. I had large egregious wounds. I had guilt. I had judgment. I had three sons. I had grief. I had a husband. I had a broken heart.

I looked over at Mary. *Let it be unto me*, she had said, simply accepting.

I thought of a folk song I liked about Mary, the one that said she was covered in roses, covered in ashes, covered in babies, covered in slashes, covered in ruins and secrets, wilderness and stains. The song reminded me that Mary's surrender had been hard won, that she had labored for it. It made me think of giving birth—that some of it was bearing down as hard as you could, but there came a moment toward the end when you had to let go and just let the birth unfold as it would.

Looking up at this Mary, I opened my own hands unconsciously in imitation of hers.

Let it be unto me, I said, *my slashes, my ashes, my babies, my olives, my ruins.*

44

A FRIEND ONCE TOLD ME THAT WHEN SHE HAD HER first child, she and her husband decided they could not go there, *there* being any conversation about things they could have done if they didn't have a baby, or any kind of reminiscing about the old days.

Having a baby was complicated. Some people regretted the choice or the circumstances that led them to become a parent, although most people would *not go there* even in the quiet of their own hearts, let alone speak aloud of regrets and losses.

Even for me, who consistently adored being a parent, motherhood was an invasion right from the start. Long before my ribcage was filled with feet seeking purchase, before I even knew there was a baby, I was taken over by fatigue, by emotion, by nausea, by cravings, by aversions.

If mine had been unwanted pregnancies, I could only imagine the terror, the panic of knowing cells were rapidly dividing, the reality every moment becoming more real, the hard choices, the uncertainty of support, the entertaining of various possible futures—dream and nightmare versions of every choice, futures that would be closed like doors, doors that could never be opened again, and new doors that could never close.

I knew deeply that no one could fully grasp the particular range of factors involved in another person's situation.

But oddly, ironically, I never understood this as well as I did when my own perfect plans for my adult children erupted with something so entirely unwanted that it made me throw up and cry, the cells of truth dividing and multiplying in my mind, my heart, and if I'm honest, deep in my belly.

45

SALVIA HAD SAID THAT CYPRESSES WERE TREES OF GRIEF, but they persisted in seeming beautiful and hope-filled to me, reaching straight into the sky. Cypresses were the trees that surrounded the place where Honey and I had sunbathed at the convent. They stood like sentinels, like angels protecting. Maybe they weren't so much trees of grief, but trees *for* grief, trees that could hold a person up in grief.

I was ready to read Jackson's letter, but I couldn't read it among the whispers and footsteps of the church. I walked outside into the brilliant afternoon sunshine, and I knew I couldn't read it surrounded by the laughter and noise of the tourists taking selfies and eating picnics on the wide *belvedere* outside San Miniato. I looked around for a quieter corner and saw that the gate to the cemetery was open and there were cypresses within it.

The San Miniato Cemetery was unlike any one I had seen at home. In addition to the tombs and crosses and flowers left at graves, there were statues of mothers who held their faces in their hands, weeping over their lost children. There were statues of young lovers, reunited in death, statues of angels on bended knees, statues of children being encircled by their mother's skirts.

The cemetery was as crowded with statuary as a garden center filled with gnomes and birdbaths. As they had been in life, so the Italians buried in this cemetery were squeezed together in close proximity in death.

I wandered through the children's cemetery, complete with old photographs of those who had died. The statue of a toddling baby was hard to look at, even though the bushes on it were overgrown enough to show that, had the baby lived, he would now be an old man.

I found a small bench underneath a cypress and took Jackson's letter out of my pocket. I had texted with my kids and with Russ the whole time I'd been away, but it was all functional, loving communication where I told them about the things I saw and did, and they replied with suitable responses, and occasionally asked me logistical questions that were hard to answer at a distance.

I thought about Jackson's text from last spring, from nearly a year ago, how I hadn't been available for it. I knew even before I opened the letter that this was not going to be a question about something random or casual.

I opened the letter. It was handwritten.

I don't know how many times I've tried to write this letter. I've told myself I have to do it this time, that I have to write to you before you come home. Remember what you always used to say about a squid in the soup? Dad told me you're mad I didn't talk to you. I'm sorry. I just couldn't. I want you guys to be proud of me. I didn't mean to tell Dad but he called me in the middle of it with a question about taxes and asked what I was doing and I couldn't lie to him. I told him I was taking Caitlin to the doctor's and he asked what was wrong and I made him swear he wouldn't tell anyone, even you. I asked Caitlin if she wanted to go to your center but she felt weird about it and to be honest I did too. If I could do it again, I don't know if I would have done anything differently. I'm sorry if you're mad at me for saying so. It's not why Caitlin and I broke up either. I think that's why I'm okay with what happened, because when she told me, I realized she wasn't the mother of my children. Or I didn't want her to be. She's a great girl and we're still friends and she's good—she got into grad school for next year—but I don't think we want the same things in life. I guess that's everything I want to say, even if you hate me for saying it. I hope you're having a good time on your Italian adventure. It's weird to think of coming home and you won't be there yet. Dad says it's been weird too.

I love you.

Jackson

My chest felt tight as I read the letter. I had tried so hard to do the right things. I had not condemned the women who chose abortion. I had not shown videos to scare them. I had not allowed their boyfriends to force them into a decision that was not what the women wanted. I had supported them whatever they chose. I had talked about birth control and not simply abstinence. I had been realistic. I had been sympathetic. I had been passionate. I had been loving. I had been compassionate.

But my family had seen me as judge and jury, and had assumed I would find them guilty. Jackson and Russ thought I was angry at them.

I remembered the weird rubber bracelets, the WWJD bracelets—what would Jesus do? I thought of Honey and her question about what Pinocchio would do. I had tried to do what I thought Jesus would do, but now I wasn't so sure.

I read the letter again. It was true that I had been angry, that I had felt sorrow at the decision, that I could not be as calm and dispassionate as I hoped I could be. But what I really felt was pain at being so unknown to them.

I read the letter again. At least Jackson had opened the door to me. At least he had signed the letter with love. At least I had another chance to try harder to make things right.

Looking at my watch, I saw it was nearly time for the Vespers service. I wondered whether I would be in trouble for missing the afternoon's work, but I felt more weary than I would have if I had spent the afternoon planting the garden. I folded up the letter and stood up and went back inside the church. There were few spaces left in the crypt on a busy afternoon, but one of the pair of women I regularly saw patted the seat beside her and moved over so there was space for me. I sat down and let the singing wash over me.

The monk with the Birkenstocks, who had also been among those who planted the baby olive trees at the convent, came out from behind the screen and stood in front of the assembled group of tourists and nuns. They stood and lined up in front of them for communion.

I had observed for weeks but this time I went forward as well, even though I was fairly sure that in doing so I was breaking some Catholic rule. It might be more like something Pinocchio would do but even though I wasn't sure exactly what I was doing, I knew why. I knew my brokenness, my need. I watched the people in front of me to see whether they crossed themselves, whether they took the wafer in their hands or let the monk give it to them.

I stood right in front of the monk, carrying my sorrow and everything with me as the count had once carried his head up the hill. I wondered whether the monks had seen me these fifty days, had seen me come to the crypt nearly as often as they had, had recognized me when we planted the new trees together at the convent. The monk offering communion held out a wafer and I let him put it in my mouth, and then I went back to sit down.

There was no wine. Just the wafer like an ice cream cone, sticking to my teeth. It was all mysterious.

Either the communion wafer awoke something in my stomach or maybe it was just the easing of tension from reading Jackson's letter. Either way, as I descended from the church after the service ended, I felt very hungry, especially after missing lunch. It would only be another hour until the nuns served one of their daily feasts, and yet I looked longingly down at the food trucks and carts parked in the Piazzale Michelangelo. As I did so, my eye fell on the replica statue of the David.

I thought of the question I had asked at the beginning of my trip, in the Accademia, about the female equivalent of the David. Something circled around and within me. Maybe it was the music of the monks or maybe it was the roof of the Duomo, the buses that circled the city, the hot milk mixing every morning in my *caffè*, me walking around the David in the Accademia, or the Vespas tracing the roundabouts. I circled and was circled and the Renaissance and the present circled and the convent library book that said God's Spirit was a motion of love circling between the Father and the Son and spiraling outward into all creation. The bells encircling the valley with their chimes, the olive oil in a small bowl, the ball of cheese at supper, the whole world.

Now I realized that the equivalent of the David was not the Venus de Milo at all, but Mary, and not Mary as the image of the perfect woman, as the perfect mother.

That wasn't how I had come to see her. For me, Mary was no longer someone on a pedestal, but someone very human, very real, someone whose love and sorrows I could understand.

I thought of the *Pietà* in the Duomo Museum that had stunned me. I understood now what I had recognized in her was the powerlessness of her humanity. She had been powerless to rescue her son. *My soul magnifies the Lord*, she had said, back when everything was new, back when she hadn't yet been made real by love. *Let it be to me*, she had said. That was the Mary who was magnificent and praised, the good mother. But the mother in the *Pietà*? It wasn't her fault, this mother, and she hadn't been able to stop it when the Flood hit. What she could do was pick up his lifeless body and hold him. She could grieve.

I had asked the wrong question in justifying myself: it wasn't so much a question of what Jesus would do, but what Mary would do.

I had always been told at my church that Catholics worshipped Mary, that they saw her wrongly, idolatrously, that they *prayed* to Mary. When my former boss had cancer, she obeyed her doctor's orders, like a nice lady, until it seemed that things weren't working, and then she broke loose, wanting to live, cracking out of her niceness—and she tried what she called voodoo treatments. She was no longer simply obedient—she was past that. I felt like I was past the cautions when it came to Mary. I came back again and again to the images of Mary, her powerful lap holding her broken son, her sorrowful face, her hands open. The Mary who knew what I knew.

As I wended my way slowly down the hill, I thought of another picture I had seen at the Leonardo da Vinci Museum, in a traveling exhibition. It was a drawing of Leonardo's called *The Cartoon of Ste Anne*, and it showed an older woman holding a younger one in her lap, the younger woman focused on her baby boy, while another child played at their feet. The younger woman was Mary, and the older was her mother, Saint Anne. I had spent a long time in front of that picture—I had never before thought about Mary having a mother. In the drawing, Anne looks at Mary and it struck me that Anne didn't know that Jesus would end up broken in Mary's lap, but she knew something of what it was to be loving and powerless, to have your child turn away from you to their own concerns.

I thought about my own mother, my conservative Baptist mother, who had worried I would become a nun if I stayed in a convent. I had rolled my eyes at her small view of Catholics, her small view of me, and now I saw her differently, as Anne who knew what it was to worry and to suffer as a powerless mother. Me going to the convent was not on the same level as Jackson's lost child—and even my mother would say so if I ever got up the nerve to tell her about the abortion—and yet she knew the pain of a child choosing something that felt frightening.

Anne was part of the furniture for Mary as my own mother was to me, and so I was to my boys. Mom loves gardening, they said, and she's going on a gardening adventure. They had summed me up as: Mom will judge abortion as wrong so we won't tell her.

Now I realized that wasn't all. Yes, they had summed me up, but I had summed myself up too. I had mistaken myself for being a mother. I'd fallen squarely into the trap of believing being a mother was entirely who I was or at least the most important part of who I was. I had come to believe that meant I needed to be the perfect mother, tangling my identity with my boys, feeling guilty and responsible for them and their actions if I wasn't perfect. That was the self I had shown to the boys and even to Russ. No wonder they had not known me. I had not known myself.

I had taken Mary off the pedestal. Now I needed to step off myself.

46

WHEN TIMOTHY WAS BORN, I DON'T know whether it was hormones or the exhilaration of the wild ride of childbirth, but I felt invincible, that I could do anything.

And yet it didn't last, and within days fears crept in. His umbilical cord stump was so unexpected and strange, and I pictured it falling off prematurely and Timmy flying around like a balloon deflating in the air. The first time I trimmed his tiny nails, the size of a grain of barley, I caught the skin on two of his fingers, cutting them, making him bleed. His latch on my nipples was poor at first and I needed my midwife to help reposition him for days.

When we came to the end of the six weeks of midwifery care, I listed my parental crimes to Virginia, my midwife. Underneath my words, were these: "You can't leave me with a baby, I'm really an amateur, more of a mother's-helper type, better at chasing toddlers than keeping infants alive."

Virginia smiled her own beatific smile. She had no doubt heard this all before.

"It's time for me to tell you a few secrets," she said, pouring me one last pottery mug of raspberry leaf tea. "First of all, what Timothy needs is a good enough mother. That's all he needs. And you, my dear, are good enough. And here's the other secret: your baby is far more resilient than he seems. Even when things go wrong, you can remind yourself that his story isn't finished yet. Your job is just to love him."

Virginia's words resettled me. I didn't feel invincible but neither did I feel like a failure. Good enough was a good goal and I fell in love with my babies and did my best.

Over time, motherhood shifted from the all-too-real physicality of bodily fluids—poop! breastmilk! pee! snot! tears!—to deeper issues. Big kids, big problems, Joanna would say. But Virginia's words still applied.

I remembered to apply Virginia's secrets when Gil fell off the swings in our backyard, when Jackson needed stitches after a dog bite at the park, when Tim dislocated his shoulder in football. The words were harder to believe as the stakes became less physical and more emotional—when Tim wasn't chosen as valedictorian, when Jackson's first girlfriend dumped him. Then I was afraid, wanting to make it all better, forgetting their resilience and that good enough was good enough, that my job was just to love them.

47

THE GUIDEBOOK CALLED IT "WISTERIA HYSTERIA," and the nuns took the season seriously enough that not only did they serve dinner in the garden on the day it bloomed but they changed their usual Sunday trip to the Pinocchio Park to visit the Bardini Gardens where they told me there was a tunnel of wisteria.

Wisteria was the English name for the *glicine*, the thousand-year-old plant that stretched along the wall of the convent near where we had burned the olive branches. It had looked like a dead branch when I arrived, and now I could see why Niccolò had been so protective of it. It was stunningly beautiful with long, lavish tendrils of purple flowers. Its fragrance was an exquisite combination of freesia and hyacinth and lilacs, fresh and floral and strong.

Something about that abundance made me feel I was ready to face Elora now. I texted her and asked her to meet me near the wisteria tunnel in the Bardini Gardens after work. It might have been more fitting to have met her again in the Loggia where the Medici and the other city fathers had met to deliberate matters of justice, but I was so conscious of how little time I had left in this city and so aware of how much I would miss its beauties, and especially the natural beauty, the gardens, and the people. The wisteria at the Bardini, I was told, was trained over a metal structure you could walk through and was at its peak. I would see Elora and the wisteria at the same time.

Part of me wondered whether in a place of such natural beauty, Elora might be wooed in a garden as I had been by the violets at the convent, whether such a place might call upon her better angels. But my main reason was simply that in my waning time in the city, I didn't want to miss the opportunity to be enveloped in the sweetness, to walk under a profusion of beauty.

I remembered so clearly when I met Elora for the first time, and now I knew I would be meeting her for the last time.

I found the lower entrance to the garden, which looked like a storefront, paid my admission, mounted two flights of stairs, stepped outdoors, and found myself at the bottom of a nearly vertical garden built on the side of a long, steep hill.

I couldn't quite bring myself to regret swearing at Elora as I had: she deserved anger for what constituted identity theft. I also didn't know how she would respond, whether she even cared about my having blown up at her: she clearly operated on a different ethical plane.

I looked for the wisteria tunnel. As I came up another flight of stairs—this one guarded by a pair of reclining statues and covered with cracked mosaic tiles—I could see a metal skeleton of a tunnel, although this one was covered in roses. Ahead of me was a steep central stairway that was blocked to the public, while to my left a gravel pathway bisected the garden, running diagonally up the steep hill. I followed the gravel path past peach and apple and cherry trees on my right.

My rage toward Elora was spent, redirected to where it more truly belonged. In its place, I felt a sense of foolishness when I thought about Elora. We were never friends before, and why had I thought we would be friends here and now? Had I wanted so badly to be wanted? To have someone embrace me rather than push me away? If so, what had I been oblivious to? I thought of the customs agents in the German airport, how they had to determine what was true and what was false, and how, similarly, I needed to retrieve and listen to my own intuition. I had been careful, wary enough of pickpockets, carried my purse carefully, avoided eye contact with the street vendors with their imitation leather and jewelry and art. I had been proud of my savvy, my self-sufficiency. But I had been so caught up in staying on my pedestal that I had fallen for Elora's deception.

I thought of the young women I'd seen sitting on broken lawn chairs on the side of the road near Matilda's castles, the migrant women, sex-trafficked on the truck route. That had surprised me. Their fates had probably surprised them, too: Honey had heard about them and had told me that many of them had come to Italy for a better life—*la dolce vita*—and likely were tricked by false friends as I had been tricked by Elora. I thought of Pinocchio and the friends who promised that coins planted in The Field of Miracles would yield a money-growing tree.

Unlike Pinocchio or the migrant women, I reminded myself that, mercifully, I had not suffered for this crime. I didn't want to think what would have happened if I had slipped and fallen while pruning trees when my health insurance card was missing. It hadn't happened but it could have, and I would have been vulnerable to Elora's theft.

At the bend in the path, under trees newly in leaf was a small bench, and then as I turned to my right, seemingly out of nowhere, the wisteria tunnel appeared. It was, as Niccolò had said, *magnifico*.

I forgot why else I had come, and I simply walked under the tunnel with its cascades of fragrant flowers, each blossom shaped like a purple teardrop, and each one giving off the most distinctive and still subtle fragrance. I walked slowly all the way to the top of the tunnel to where it joined a small olive grove on one side and a lookout on the other, and then I walked slowly back down the hill where I settled myself on the bench and waited for Elora.

Within a few minutes, I saw her coming up the diagonal hill near the fruit trees, her hands on her thighs with the effort of climbing the steep hill. I remembered the story she'd told me at Canossa about the king who had come penitent before the Pope, walking up a mountain in winter in his bare feet, to be restored for his sin. I was no pope, had no absolution to offer. This was anything but winter, and there was no contrition in Elora. I could see that by the way she walked.

She was dressed in her customary shapeless black layered garments and wore her hair in its severe black bob. I wondered how she had managed to persuade a doctor that she was me, based on the photo on my health insurance. Or perhaps the doctor had winked too. I could not see Elora's eyes; they were covered by black sunglasses so opaque I wondered whether she could even see the dappled light of the wisteria through them.

She reminded me of so many young women I had known who had tried to draw me into the drama of their pregnancy. I knew to draw boundary lines—"Not my circus, not my monkeys"—even if I'd sometimes forgotten to do so. I was doing it now. Russ might be my circus, and our sons my monkeys, but I owed nothing to Elora.

As she drew closer, I could see, despite her sunglasses, that she looked understandably cautious. I realized I did have something to give to her.

"Thanks for meeting me," I said, standing up from the bench from which I had been surveying the city, all the while breathing in the fragrance of the flowers around me. "I'm not going to curse you out again. I'm sorry about that."

A muscle twitched in her jaw. I remembered the little girl in the exotic print, the clogs, the girl who could talk to dead Elvis.

"I wanted to say a few things now that I'm coherent," I said. "Do you want to sit down?"

"I don't need a lecture," she said, and she sat and folded her arms across her chest. I sat down beside her.

"It's not that. It's this. If you had told me that you needed surgery, that you needed to have a cyst removed, I would have gladly given you some money to help out. All you had to do was ask."

She whistled air through her teeth. "I told you before—this was just working the system. I didn't need charity. I just needed Canada to remember me a little, to pay one lousy bill so I wouldn't be dying in pain."

"You're feeling better?"

She raised an eyebrow above her glasses. "I am. Thanks." There was sarcasm in her voice.

"I also wanted to let you know I'm not going to report you."

"Report me?"

"To the insurance company or the police." I had decided not to tell Russ either; he might be obligated as an employee of the insurance company to say something. I wouldn't lie but I would do what I could to avoid an explanation, to hope it was chalked up as a clerical error.

She swore under her breath, shaking her head.

"But," I said, "this is the end. I wish you well and I'm glad you're feeling better, but I realize now we were never friends."

"How can you say I'm not your friend? I took you to see the castles."

I took a breath. Maybe she believed this. It wasn't my definition of friendship, nor was her using my card, taking it from my wallet while I was in her home.

"*Ciao, bella*," she said, standing up. She turned and began down the path again, not even waiting for my reply.

Not my circus, I said to myself as I walked the other direction up through the wisteria tunnel again, a warm breeze enveloping me. At the other end was the small olive grove. I could see that some of the trees needed pruning to be fruitful, that a bird would not be able to fly through the branches of some of these trees. I could also see small gardens in beds formed into concentric circles, into a kind of labyrinth, like the one I had walked at the retreat center last fall. I didn't step into this labyrinth, but with a finger in the air I traced its pathway, remembering what the sign at the retreat center last fall had said, that you could trust a labyrinth, that it was not a maze with dead ends—you would find your way through if you followed the path.

I had let Elora walk away without taking on what she had done. I let her go. I walked on and looked out from the *belvedere* to the city far below. I walked on and there was a long artificial waterway. I followed it and found its source, a fountain with water coming out of the mouth of a stone lion. I briefly considered taking my shoes off and stepping into the fountain but having just dismissed the idea of contacting the authorities about Elora's crime, I didn't relish the thought of being arrested for public nuisance in my last week in Florence.

I did let the water splash over my fingers, washing Elora from my hands.

As I walked down the hill to the villa on the side of the garden, I thought of another phrase we used in the center—*fool me once, shame on you; fool me twice, shame on me.* I had beaten myself up for being fooled by Elora because my trust had already been damaged by the boys and especially Russ.

Now I realized two things: I had not responded the same way this time. I had raged instead of being broken by someone else's choices. I had not taken it on, not tried to fix it. I had named it as wrong this time. This time, I had changed.

The squid in the soup. Now I needed to do that naming with Russ too, to truly speak it out, to show him who I was and what I needed.

The second thing was nearly the opposite. I had not been a fool, as I'd said to Honey. I had been myself, both with my family and with Elora. Maybe I had run away instead of facing things. Maybe I had made it about me when it never was. Maybe I had missed the crucial text. Maybe I had judged them. But I also knew I had done the best I could and that was what it meant to step off the pedestal, to stop endlessly second-guessing myself and expecting perfection. It was enough to be me.

Outside the Bardini Villa stood lemon trees in pots. They gave me a sense of déjà vu until I remembered my dream from the night before. I dreamed that I was pregnant and that the nuns had wrapped me in the burlap they used to wrap the lemon trees in the *limonaia* and told me I was safe and secure. And then I was a baby in the burlap.

There was a little bench under the lemon trees. I sat on the bench, in the scent of their waxy white blossoms, and wrote an email to Jackson. This time I did not write in cheerful perfect Mom language. I did not explain myself or ask him to explain himself. I simply told him that I loved him, that he was so dearly loved no matter what. It was all he needed to hear. It was all I needed to say.

Now as I stepped out through the gate at the bottom of the Bardini Gardens and into the city, I squared my shoulders. For the first time in months, I felt as though I could breathe deeply. I looked back at the garden I had just emerged from, and thought of the wisteria tunnel, feeling reborn and ready to face the world, my life.

48

THE FIRST EASTER AFTER MY DAD DIED WE STAYED with my mom so that she wouldn't be alone. My mom didn't "do" the Easter bunny, as we had the year before with Timothy, though I was fairly sure my now two-year-old wouldn't remember either way. But I brought a small bag of chocolate eggs and planned to hide them around Timothy's room before he woke up. Jackson was three months old, and I knew he would wake me in the night to feed; I would hide the eggs then, I decided.

When I woke up in the night, the house was quiet. Russ was not in bed beside me, nor was the baby in the basket we had brought for him to sleep in. I was instantly wide awake. I couldn't imagine I had slept through his cries while Russ hadn't. I crept down to the rec room, the most remote part of the house, expecting to see them, but they weren't there. I looked out the front window—we had occasionally taken a crying baby for a drive to settle him—and our car was still parked in the driveway. I tiptoed back up the stairs in the split level, and checked in on Timothy, who was sound asleep, thumb in mouth, in the bed that had once been mine. Still no Russ or Jackson. Had he taken the baby for a midnight walk?

I looked out the window and there was Russ, standing in the backyard, baby in a carrier on his chest, stirring a pot over my father's cookstove.

I hurried back to our bedroom, threw on a sweater and shoes, and went into the yard. The air was cool and damp and it smelled surprisingly of applewood smoke.

"What the heck are you doing?" I whispered, quiet in the night.

Russ put a finger to his lips. "I'm making maple syrup. It was supposed to be a surprise. I took the baby so it could be a surprise, so you could get some sleep."

Jackson began rooting in the carrier, and I felt my milk begin to let down, and also tears.

Russ hadn't said a lot to me about my dad's death. Russ was a practical guy, not a feelings guy—my dad was dead and we couldn't bring him back so what was there to say? Russ spoke up when my male cousins assumed that, as men, they should take on the role usually assumed by children in our family, giving the eulogy at their parents' funeral. Russ said that I was capable of speaking. When I was unsure whether I could actually do it, Russ sat in the church, eyes on me, as I spoke about my dad and how much I loved him. But in the weeks after that we had been busy with the baby and the toddler and just functioning, and I assumed Russ thought I had enough on my plate, that I should let the grief go. I had felt alone in my sorrow.

I went to the shed and found the lawn chairs my dad and I had sat in to make maple syrup. I unfolded them, sat in one and patted the other, inviting Russ to sit in it.

"Don't I have to keep stirring?" he said.

I took the wooden paddle from him and gave the mixture a stir. The air was smoky and sweet. I held the paddle out of the kettle for a minute to let it cool and then I tasted a bit of the syrup.

"We have time," I said. "It needs watching but we still have time." I reached for the baby and took him out of the carrier. He was warm and soft and small. I hadn't dressed to feed him outside but it was three in the morning so I didn't think the neighbors would be appalled if I hoisted up my nightgown.

The moon was just past full, as it always was at Easter, my dad had once explained to me. It was because Easter fell during Passover, it was during the Passover feast that Jesus was betrayed, and Passover was always connected with the full moon so the Jews could walk up to Jerusalem safely by night.

I sat in the chair and settled the baby at my breast. Russ got up and stirred the syrup again. I felt amazed and confused and loved. "Where did you get the sap from?" I asked.

"I asked a Mennonite guy at work if I could buy a bucket of sap from him. I brought it here the other day."

Russ was infinitely practical, and while he often messed up, lost when it came to feelings and words, sometimes they showed up in unexpected, sweet ways.

We would have about a cup of syrup from the sap. It would be thinner than my dad usually made it, but it would be sweet and we would eat it on pancakes when Timothy and my mom woke up. All day long I would look over at Russ and realize that sometimes, once in a while, we could find one another again even when I wasn't sure we could.

49

Weeks before, Patrizia and Elora had said that the change might be abrupt, that spring itself might come at any time, but that the influx of tourists came predictably in Holy Week, the week before Easter, as though they were migratory birds or butterflies that could be counted on.

What I didn't count on was that it would be a sea change, that the city would be utterly transformed as the week leading up to Easter began. Elora had once said it was a small world, but now it began to feel like the whole world had come to Florence. Even the convent was full, every table in the dining room entirely filled with tourists. I heard English all around me.

Every morning, Kaito and Sora joined Niccolò and me working in the gardens, and even the gardens were not quiet. Arborists in a brightly colored van arrived to trim the topiary bushes in the garden, and the whine and whirr of their various tools and the sound of the music they blasted filled the air. Then, too, as we broke the surface of the soil of the vegetable garden with the hoes Niccolò had given us, some of the tourists inevitably came out to the gardens, mostly to take photos of the wisteria, which was now past its peak but still beautiful. They would stop to ask where the wisteria was, and to ask where we were from, how long we had worked at the convent, and what we were planting. It was complicated to explain where the wisteria was so I would often lead little groups to see it, feeling like a tour guide, carrying my hoe instead of a peacock feather, explaining that it was called *glicine*, that it was a thousand years old, taking the requisite group shots with their cameras in front of it.

Niccolò brought flats of coral geraniums for us to nestle into the large terracotta planters, and flats with smaller cells of vegetable seedlings to be planted in the vegetable garden, along with packets of seeds. He had a diagram and he explained it to Sora in Italian and left it with her to direct us while he checked on the arborists and determined which herbs in the herb garden would need replacing. It felt like an unexpectedly busy time in the garden, like the week before a big celebration, which I suppose, it was. No longer was I anti-gardening: I was planting new seeds and plants. Perhaps that was cause for celebration too.

It was strange to plant a garden I would not eat from. I had eaten from it while I was there—zucchini and garlic and potatoes throughout my visit—and the vegetables I planted would send their roots down into the ground, grow and be harvested by future volunteers, and cooked in the kitchen and served to people who came after me.

Salvia came out to the garden late on Tuesday morning to tell me her mother had died and she was going home for the funeral. She came to say goodbye.

"*Dio ti benedica*, Elizabetta," she said. "God bless you."

I stood up and wiped off the dirt from my hands. "Can I hug you?" I asked, and she let me put my arms around her, like wings around a small bird. "Thank you," I said to her. "God bless you too."

I wondered whether the *Madre* would have words with me about hugging her, but no one came out so I began poking holes into the soil again, and sprinkling carrot seeds in them. The soil at my house was loose and sandy; the soil at the convent was a rich, dark, loamy brown. It was crusted at the surface from dryness, but otherwise, it was like a bag of soil from a garden center, only requiring us to loosen it. The day we burned the branches, Niccolò explained to Honey and me that every fall when the olives were pressed for oil, he would bring the residue back and mix it into the vegetable garden. I lifted a clod of earth to my nose and wondered if I could smell the olives, but all I was sure of was that it didn't smell like the soil in my garden.

Because I would somehow, impossibly, be home again by the end of the week, my afternoons after work were equally busy as I headed out into the crowds in the city to go shopping. As I looked in vain for the bitter *tabacchi* woman in the now-full piazza, and fought my way past hordes on the Ponte Vecchio, I thought of Honey, who wished she'd gone home before we spread manure around the trees. For my part, I wished I'd known that there would have been such an invasion of tourists as I would have at least done my shopping before this last week of my *avventura*.

Early on in my trip, I had seen graffiti painted on a wall: David as twenty-first-century tourist, complete with cell phone, sunglasses, an *I ♥ Florence* tee shirt, and an entitled look on his face. It had been funny to me back when the streets of Florence were quieter—I took a picture and sent it to Joanna—but at Peak Tourist now it was less amusing. It was clearly spring break somewhere, or maybe everywhere. The streets were filling with tourists, much like the Arno had filled the city in the flood of 1966. This time the students, like the graffitied *David*, were less saviors of art, and more out for selfies.

Gone were the art hawkers from the street. In their place were seasonal workers: caricature artists, mimes dressed as statues, watercolor artists painting the Ponte Vecchio while sitting in fold-up chairs, carts now filled with World Cup jerseys and postcards and a thousand Pinocchios.

For weeks, I'd seen shop windows begin to fill with Easter eggs as though they were jewels. Chocolate stores had displays of Easter eggs and so did more unexpected stores—even the smallest *tabacchi* had little Easter designs in the windows, and big chocolate eggs intricately decorated with exquisite icing ducks and chicks and rabbits.

I had planned to buy chocolate eggs to bring back for the boys, but as I walked through the streets, I thought of how I would have to pack the chocolate, and I realized that I could bring back chocolate shards, or chocolate that had melted en route, but I was unlikely to be able to carry an egg back intact to my family.

I would have to tell Russ where to buy chocolate to hide on Easter morning, and then I said the words *mental load* to myself, a reminder that if Russ had managed to keep himself and the cats alive for seven weeks—and he apparently had—he could make the decisions about what to do for Easter. I stopped and texted him, asking him to take care of it, and telling him I wanted to talk with him about the squid in the soup when I got back. He wrote back: *I'm glad you're coming home.*

On Thursday afternoon, I found the address I had tried to find for several days. I had expected a storefront—possibly with Easter eggs in it—but the entire block near the train station was apparently all office buildings. It must have moved, I nearly decided, and then a door opened and I was surrounded by the smell of a thousand flowers. I stopped and looked at the address. Although it looked just the same as every other office building, it in fact bore the number of the shop I was seeking. I grabbed the door before it swung shut and I stepped inside where the scent was even stronger, feeling as though I was stepping into a real-life fairy tale.

The foyer was like an Easter egg itself, tiled mosaics hidden inside the most pedestrian of exteriors. I followed several women who seemed to know exactly what they were doing, up several old marble stairs and into a larger hallway and then into an inner chamber.

I'd read about this shop in my guidebook: it had been part of a monastery, and its products were still largely made from medieval recipes. The main room was large, and its ceiling was vaulted like a small, private cathedral. It opened onto other rooms, and I walked through them, wondering whether every office door on the block hid other wonders. There was even a small courtyard between the apothecary room that was filled with medicinal herbs and a tearoom. I walked quietly, my hands behind my back, simply breathing in the smells.

When I returned to the first room, I watched as a woman with long blonde hair and a Texas drawl handed over her credit card and received a heavy paper bag of purchases from an attendant behind one of the glass counters.

There were product lists at intervals along the counters, between samples of the various products. I saw that you made your choices and then an attendant would find what you had chosen and bring it to you to pay for it. I ran a finger down the list—there were so many exotic smells and, if it had not been for the exorbitant prices, like the Texan, I would have been tempted to choose one of everything.

Then I saw it: violet-scented soap. In my mind, I flashed to the afternoon in the garden, surrounded by violets, being wooed, being aware that I was loved not as mother, not as wife, not as executive director, but as myself.

I pointed to the soap I wanted on the menu, and the woman returned with it. It was small and egg-shaped and wrapped in white paper with simple black writing, and when I held it to my nose, I was back in the garden once more, sitting in the grass on the hillside, my olive trees newly pruned below me, the wisteria about to open into luxurious bloom, as content as a green lizard in the sunshine.

I carried it back to the convent in my hand, walking the entire way, soaking in the sights and sounds and smells of the city, laughing as I came upon the impossible lineups of tourists in the piazza of the Duomo. Crossing the Arno, I thought back to the movie *A Room with a View* where I had first seen images of Florence. I thought about how the characters had thrown the postcards stained by the blood of the murdered man into this river to be washed away. I thought about how the Arno had risen to swamp the city with mud, and how people had swum it with manuscripts in their teeth. I remembered my idea of throwing my whistle into the Arno. I thought about how the river flowed to the Mediterranean, past the Pinocchio Park where I had spoken the truth that had set me free, and beyond to the Atlantic I would fly over in two days.

I walked up the hill to the convent and was buzzed inside where I could smell lasagna cooking. Should I tell Russ to get a ham for Easter? I lifted the violet soap to my nose and let the thought go.

In Lemonland I was alone—other than the portrait of Mary on my wall. I opened the shutters and windows of my room and I sat on my bed, back against the wall, facing her and the dried mimosa and lightning-branches in the glass beneath the picture. I remembered I had intended to go into the English Church, just to say I'd been inside. I lifted the violet soap to my nose again. I wondered whether I should tell the women at San Miniato that I would be leaving, wondered how Honey was doing at home, and what home would be like for me, and then I stopped and listened to the sound of the birds outside—the arborists were done with their work and I could hear the birds and the bells once more.

I realized for the first time that the image on my wall was simply that of Mary. So many of the pictures of Mary were of her with baby Jesus or her holding the dead Jesus in her lap, like the *Pietà*. This was just Mary, and she was enough.

Mary looked out at me, and I looked back at her.

50

I DIDN'T KNOW WHAT WAS AHEAD OF ME BUT I HAD found out what I would miss. A pair of British guests staying at the convent, who had come to Florence for Easter, told me I had timed my leaving badly, missing Florence's special Easter tradition, the *Scoppo del Carrio.*

Every Easter for hundreds of years, the tradition had been to carry fire throughout the city on Easter Sunday, lit by flints brought back to Florence from the Crusades. Over time this evolved, and for the last five hundred years, every Easter Sunday morning, a tall antique cart was filled with fireworks and explosives and was pulled through the city by a pair of white oxen, decorated with flowers. The cart would be positioned just outside the doors of the Duomo, and a wire attached to it would be stretched inside to the high altar of the cathedral. This wire would be fitted with a mechanical dove-shaped rocket. At the conclusion of the service, while bells tolled outside, the archbishop would light the dove on fire and it would be propelled through the church and out the door, colliding with the cart and setting off the fireworks display that would explode for the next twenty minutes. The dove, meanwhile, was to return along the wire to the altar; if it did, this would be a sign of a good harvest ahead, a good year coming.

I said goodbye to the beetle-browed Mother Superior, handing her my keys, and then took a bus toward the airport. As the bus sped along and then as I went through security and handed in my suitcase at the airport, I thought of the astronomer I had met the first morning in Florence, the man who had come to study at the Galileo observatory and who had stayed at the convent. Somewhere in a church I had visited, an explosion would happen the next day, as it had happened for centuries. I had no doubt that would happen. But as I climbed on the plane on Holy Saturday, I realized that I preferred it this uncertain way, not knowing whether the dove would return.

Seated on this school bus of a plane, I trusted that it would lift me up into the air, over the Alps, and that another plane would carry me across an ocean back into my own country. I trusted that the monks in San Miniato would continue singing their Vespers as they had for a thousand years, and for fifty days. I trusted that the trees would bear olives, that the garden would grow. When I had said goodbye to Niccolò, I told him that I hoped and believed he would reach his fifty-year milestone of tending the olives.

What I did not know was what was ahead: the cat that was both alive and dead until it was proven one way or the other.

I could not prove what would happen. But traveling on Holy Saturday felt right. It was the in-between day, a good day for travel, a day between the tragedy that was Good Friday and the unexpected joy of Easter Sunday, the resurrection day.

I didn't know what was ahead of me. In my worst moments, I feared that I would return and everything would slide right back into place, that the pain would be waiting for me. It had been a long fifty days. It had been meaningful and painful. I had gained calluses and cut my hair. I had been cheated and lied to. I had been lost and found. For Russ and the boys, maybe it had been short and same-old same-old.

I didn't know whether the dove would make it back to the altar. I couldn't know. I had forgotten to check whether the lightning-struck tree had new shoots springing out of it. And even if it did, was it only superstition to think that it meant anything?

As my plane lifted into the air and I saw the Arno curving beneath me, saw the red terracotta roofs, saw as we banked the green hills on the other side of the Arno where the cypresses made a dark wood, where my olive trees still stood—even the one that had been so violently damaged—I could see more of how the pieces fit together, and I knew that new life was springing up inside of me, that it would be a good year ahead regardless of what happened. "*Allora*," I said quietly aloud, as the plane reached for altitude. "*Andiamo*." Let's go.

Later still as my plane lifted high above the Atlantic, above the whole world, I found myself picturing a young boy detaching the dove from the wire after it had flown back inside the church, like Noah when the dove returned with an olive leaf that showed the flood water had receded, that there might be resurrection, new life, a new earth.

I touched the window and I thought of Niccolò tipping the olive oil to his mouth, raising his hands to the sky and then to the trees, saying his thanks. *Grazie*, I said, and again, *grazie*.

ACKNOWLEDGMENTS

Grazie, says Liz as she leaves Italy, and *grazie* say I as this novel goes out in the world. So many thank yous.

This novel began when I saw the film *A Room with a View* on my own in a theater in Toronto and was enraptured. That spring I dressed in a white cotton dress with white lace stockings for my prom. Thank you, Mr. Forster, for the introduction. Twenty years later when my husband had an impending sabbatical and we were stuck for ideas of what to do, Florence came to mind, and so we went to Italy where we stayed in a convent called Villa Agape. *Grazie* to Florence's nuns and monks for your hospitality.

Thank you to my husband and my family. I wrote this book in anticipation of an empty nest and have been delighted our experience has been far less traumatic than Liz's. This book was accepted by two publishers: both times on the day my husband left the country. Dave, I'm so glad to have you by my side on this journey—and I'm also thankful you go away sometimes. To my kids—Matt, John, Megan—for all the adventures. I love you. Thanks also to my parents for encouraging me ever since the Charlotte and Holly story days.

Thank you to Don Pape, my longtime agent and friend who is a champion of good writers and good writing (and who is also willing to say when my writing isn't good). You love this book and worked hard to find the right home for it. All the All-Dressed potato chips are for you.

Thank you to my beloved Hopeful Writers group—Erin Bow, Kristen Mathies, Pamela Mulloy, Nan Forler, and the late Esther Regehr—who have cheered this book on and who have been dear friends and thoughtful, hopeful.

Thank you to my editor, Lil Copan. It was like Christmas morning—almost literally—to work with you on this novel. Thank you for making it so much stronger than it was.

To Paraclete Press: it was always you I wanted to work with on the publication of this book. I just had to wait until you had a fiction imprint. It takes a village—or an arts-loving ecumenical community—to make a book. Thank you to the entire Paraclete Press team for your part in making this book a reality. It has been a joy.

To Tim Underwood who not only sends me cryptic wordplays about my surname but also is behind any marketing I ever do.

To Diane Schomperlen who worked as a writing coach and editor with me on a draft of this book, to the late Jennifer Campbell-Palmateer whose approval of an early version of this book mattered to me, and to other friends and colleagues who read early drafts. Karl Kessler gave me the idea of the squid in the soup while Rebecca Sutherns often reminds me "big kids, big problems" among much other wisdom.

I'm appreciative to both the Abbey of the Arts and *The Globe and Mail* for publishing pieces about my Italy research trip.

Big thanks to Dr. Jennifer Russell for insights on trauma, and hugs and kisses to Dr. Lisa Koski who introduced us and who also told me about "the part where the scary music starts."

Grazie mille to Francesco Robles who taught me and my husband in eight weeks of Italian classes before we went to Italy. I told him my goal was full fluency and it turned out that was wise if ambitious since not one of the nuns we stayed with spoke a word of English. We weren't fluent (I mispronounced *gnocchi* to my eternal shame) but we were able to communicate, in the present tense anyhow.

Grazie to Marcus Costantino who read through the bits of English spoken by native Italian speakers and made it sound more like his grandparents' idiom than it did. I would have loved to work in your grandfather's "I, me dying" but I've used it myself instead when I've been ill.

While Liz's center is fictitious, I'm appreciative to Andrea Rennie of Monica House for showing me how a residential home for pregnant teens operates, and to Maureen Dinner, who let me interview her about what it's like to helm a pregnancy center, the misconceptions and the hard realities.

When I was deep in the writing of this book, I was working as Writer in Residence at the University of Waterloo's social entrepreneur incubator, GreenHouse. I'm so thankful for the young entrepreneurs who inspired me as they demonstrated the ability to pivot and start again.

I'm profoundly grateful to my now-retired spiritual director, Marian Wiens, who walked with me through the griefs of the end of motherhood.

I owe a debt to Brian Chatterton and the Mediterranean Garden Society's newsletter for tips on pruning olive trees. I'm also appreciative to Majla and the Accidental Tourist who taught us to make pasta and who exchanged our bottles of Canadian maple syrup for fresh olive oil that rarely makes it out of Italy.

Thanks to anyone I've forgotten. Your contributions to this book can be our secret.

And finally, *grazie* to you, dear reader. In the words of a line from the play *Shadowlands*, we read to know we are not alone. I write so that both you and I know we aren't alone. A book isn't truly done until it's been read, so thanks for being part of its creation.

ABOUT PARACLETE PRESS

PARACLETE PRESS IS THE PUBLISHING ARM of the Cape Cod Benedictine community, the Community of Jesus. Presenting a full expression of Christian belief and practice, we reflect the ecumenical charism of the Community and its dedication to sacred music, the fine arts, and the written word.

THE RAVEN, TO ANCIENT PEOPLES, represented light, wisdom, and sustenance, as well as darkness and mystery. In the same spirit, Raven Fiction reflects the whole of human experience, from the darkness of injustice, oppression, doubt, and pain to experiences of awe and wonder, hope, goodness, and beauty.

YOU MAY ALSO BE INTERESTED IN